CU00950019

Lure of the Dragon

Book 1
Aloha Shifters: Jewels of the Heart

by Anna Lowe

TWIN MOON PRESS

Copyright © 2017 Anna Lowe

All rights reserved.

Editing by Lisa A. Hollett

Covert art by Kim Killion

Contents

Other books in this series

Aloha Shifters - Jewels of the Heart

Lure of the Dragon (Book 1)

Lure of the Wolf (Book 2)

Lure of the Bear (Book 3)

Lure of the Tiger (Book 4)

Love of the Dragon (Book 5)

visit www.annalowebooks.com

Free Books

Get your free e-books now!

Sign up for my newsletter at *annalowebooks.com* to get three free books!

- *Desert Wolf*: Friend or Foe (Book 1.1 in the Twin Moon Ranch series)

- *Off the Charts* (the prequel to the Serendipity Adventure series)

- *Perfection* (the prequel to the Blue Moon Saloon series)

Chapter One

Tessa took two shaky steps toward the ornate gate of the private driveway and stopped. Was she really going to do this?

You can trust them, Ella had said. Ella, the neighbor who'd come along at exactly the right moment and saved her life.

Tessa bit her lip. The fabric at the shoulder of her shirt was ripped, and her throat ached from the attack. Her fingers were still shaking, and her mind was haunted by visions of a terrifying beast. How could she trust anyone after what had happened less than twenty-four hours before?

You have to trust them. No one else can protect you from that monster.

Crickets chirped from the lush foliage, and a bat flew overhead, a splotch of black against the dark night. Palms swayed in the tropical breeze, echoing Ella's words. *No one else. There's no one else.*

Tessa shivered in spite of the balmy night, unwilling to trust her own senses. Sure, the sea was whispering over the shore in a reassuring way. And yes, the moon's rippling reflection over the Pacific should be soothing, like the sweet scent of hibiscus. But even the island paradise of Maui could try to deceive her. Nightmares could break the deepest peace — real-life nightmares she couldn't block out of her memory no matter how hard she tried. She could still see the glowing eyes of the creature that had attacked her.

Mine. You will be mine, his voice boomed in her mind.

She drew a deep breath and looked over her shoulder, wishing she hadn't sent the taxi away. The past twenty-four hours had been a whirlwind. She'd barely slept, and fear pulsed

1

through her veins like poison. How could she possibly judge whom to trust?

She tipped her head back at the stars and gulped. She was alone at night in a remote corner of Maui, far off the beaten track, about to knock on the door of a complete stranger for help.

A very rich stranger, she decided, inspecting the gate. There was an elaborate design in the middle, but she couldn't quite make it out. Something swirly. Toothy. Wait — was that a tail? Shit, was it a dragon, or was she seeing things?

She shook the thought away and told herself to think. A gate that massive must protect a hell of an estate — a seaside estate in Maui that had made the taxi driver whistle when she gave the address back at the airport.

"Koa Point Estate," he'd said. "You've got the right friends, miss."

Tessa gnawed on her lip. These weren't friends. They were complete strangers. And anyway, the man who'd attacked her in Phoenix was rich, too. Rich didn't mean trustworthy — or even human.

A tremor went through her at the memory of her attacker's fingernails turning into claws and reaching out for her.

Mine. You will be mine.

Tessa shook her head and turned back for the road. Who knew what secrets lay behind that gate? It would be safer to head back to Lahaina and find a hotel for the night. After a good night's sleep, she could—

The beams of twin headlights blinded her, and a powerful engine purred into the driveway. Tessa froze as a vintage Jaguar approached then stopped. For a moment, nothing happened, and Tessa considered whether to run, but her legs stayed rooted to the spot.

The driver's door opened, and a tall man climbed out. Tessa squinted against the lights, trying to make out his face as he stood silently inspecting her for a full minute.

"Have you decided yet?" His deep voice boomed, making her jump.

Tessa clutched her bag to her chest. "Who are you?"

He stepped forward, and a tiny grin formed at one corner of his mouth. "Who are you?"

Tessa tried to form an answer, but her lips were shaking, as was the rest of her body. Was this man a potential ally or a deadly foe?

His dark hair and bright blue eyes contrasted with the pure white of his dress shirt, open at the neck. Sharp, angled features cast their own sub-shadows over his face. Tall and imposing, he seemed perfectly at home in the night.

Vampire, her subconscious screamed. *He must be a vampire.*

Tessa discarded the idea a second later. Surely a vampire would give her creepy vibes. Despite the fine cut of his clothes, this man exuded an untamed, animal feel, like a lion or a wolf. A predator just as capable of ripping an enemy limb from limb as he was of protecting the one he loved.

A little shiver went down her spine.

Tessa tried to shake the feeling off and collected her thoughts. She doubted he was a vampire. Ella had sent her to a band of shapeshifters, right?

"I'm Tessa. Tessa Byrne."

She hadn't intended to give her full name, but damn. There was something fiercely commanding about the man — that, and he was so blindingly handsome, even in the dimness of night — that her brain had short-circuited.

"So, Tessa," he murmured like a man savoring a new brandy. "Have you decided yet?"

"Decided what?" she asked, taking another step back.

"Whether you're coming or going."

Coming, part of her brain said. The part that couldn't help noticing the ripple of muscles under the thin fabric of his shirt.

Going, the terrified part of her soul screeched. *Go, quick.*

But she didn't move. She couldn't. Or maybe she didn't *want* to, because that might mean losing sight of him — and being alone when instinct screamed at her to stay.

"I'm... I'm not sure." God, she hated being indecisive. Her whole life she had been confident, capable, and strong. But ever since she'd been attacked by something not-quite-human, she didn't know where she stood anymore.

He stood studying her for a full minute before speaking again. A minute in which his eyes grazed over her body and his nostrils flared. A lot like her attacker had, and yet in a totally different way. For some mystifying reason, this stranger put her at ease, whereas she'd been wary of her attacker long before he'd shown his true self.

When the man locked eyes with her, her heart thumped hard and heavy, and an achy sensation set in under her ribs. An inexplicable yearning sensation, as if she'd been missing something terribly important all her life and only realized it now.

"What are you doing here?" he asked.

She shook her mind back into focus and asked herself the same thing. A gentle sea breeze kissed her cheeks, reminding her where *here* was. Maui. A speck of an island in the middle of the Pacific. Would she be safe here?

"Ella sent me. She said to come to Koa Point and ask for help. She said to explain what happened."

"And what might that be?"

"I was attacked by Damien Morgan. Last night, in Phoenix."

The words came tumbling out, and when the man didn't react, Tessa panicked. Had she said the wrong thing?

Then she realized he had gone stiff all over, and his eyes were no longer on her, but sweeping the darkness behind.

"Come with me," he said curtly, tapping a keypad beside the gate.

Fear nipped at her heels, and she hurried toward the car. His voice was that urgent, that convincing.

"Get in," he said, motioning her to the passenger seat.

His arms were so long and sculpted, she did a double take before obeying. The man was built like an Olympic swimmer — the big guys who swam butterfly, with incredibly broad shoulders and lumps of muscle along both arms. Even when he slid into the car beside her, he was pure, coiled power.

He hit a remote control, murmured something Tessa couldn't hear into a speaker, then drove in.

Tessa clutched at her leather seat, wondering if running away would have been the safer bet. But it was too late now.

The driveway was full of twists and turns, hiding the view ahead. The moon peeked from between the palms, giving her short glimpses of a varied landscape: patches of perfectly trimmed lawn between thick bamboo stands and huge, leafy bushes that whispered and swayed. One sweeping curve later, the driveway ended at a long, arched garage. It looked like a stable, making Tessa wonder how many thoroughbred engines lay slumbering inside. The man parked and stepped out of the car in one smooth motion.

"Follow me."

He motioned her down a flagstone path between lush bougainvillea and palms, following closely enough that it ought to make her nervous, yet she felt comforted instead of crowded. As if he was protecting her back, making sure she was safe.

But when they came out into a clearing lit by tiki torches, Tessa halted in her tracks. She'd been expecting a breezy mansion, perhaps with a uniformed servant or two, but what she saw was an open-sided shack with a thatched roof bristling with guards. Well, the four men there looked like guards. They were big — really big, not to mention intent and focused as she approached. They held their arms away from their sides, ready for imminent action. Like this was a war zone and not Hawaii.

Then she remembered what Ella had said. *They're Special Forces. Well, they were. Men with rough backgrounds and tough starts. But don't let them scare you. They're puppies inside.*

Tessa balked, because *Rottweiler* was a more apt description of the men before her now.

The tallest of the four stepped forward and shooed her into the building with a gravelly, "Come in."

When she hesitated, the man who'd met her at the gate nodded her forward with a gesture that said, *Don't worry. I will keep you safe.*

She might have snorted at the idea, but then she saw him glare the other men down in a distinct, *touch-her-and-you-die* stance. So she stepped forward, wondering why she trusted him already. Why she trusted any of them.

"Sit down," the tall man said. "Talk. Explain."

He was definitely military, she decided, even if the surroundings were anything but. The open-air structure resembled some luxury apartments she'd seen — the kind of place with a big, open layout, except without walls. There was a living area with four couches set in a square. A wide dining table surrounded by heavy chairs stood to one side. A designer kitchen occupied the left side of the structure, complete with an island and a rack of hanging copper pots — the kind of kitchen she would have loved to explore if she wasn't completely on edge. A huge grill took up one corner, and an oversized stainless-steel refrigerator stood beside a deep sink. The sea breeze wafted through the space since there were no walls, just posts supporting the broad roof that extended a good yard over each side.

It was a beautiful space. Simplistic yet elegant in a purely masculine way — like the ground floor of a very fancy fraternity with a tropical theme.

Tessa followed the man's gesture and sank into a deep couch — so deep, she'd never escape if they jumped her, but she barely cared any more. The second she touched the soft cushions, part of her sighed as if she'd come home. Which was stupid, plain stupid for a woman on the run.

"Get her a drink," the man from the gate growled at one of the others.

One moved to obey, which left four big, hulking men crowded around her, making her tremble. Her eyes darted from one to another, wondering whom she could trust.

Shapeshifters, Ella had told her. *Human, but not quite human.*

Tessa would have laughed the woman off if she hadn't had terrifying proof that such things were possible — like the sight of Damien Morgan morphing into a dragon.

"All right, guys," one with sandy brown hair said in a decidedly more laid-back voice. "Give her some space, already." He grinned. "Don't worry. We don't bite."

Boone, the wolf shifter, Ella's voice echoed in her mind. *He's the most outgoing one.*

Tessa pursed her lips. *Outgoing* was a relative term, because she could picture Boone snarling down an enemy just as easily as she could imagine him wagging his tail. Then she caught herself because, whoa — she really could imagine him in wolf form. There was something about the way his tousled hair fell over his eyes that made it easy to picture. Not that she'd ever seen a werewolf before. Christ, she'd never seen any shapeshifter until the previous day. She'd never believed in them, either. But now...

She glanced around. Any of the five men clustered around her could have featured in a calendar of Hawaiian Hunks or Muscled Marines. But now that the world of shapeshifters had been revealed to her, she could see their second sides, too. She craned her neck, curious about the dark-haired man from the gate. But he was standing behind her — protecting her from the others, or cutting off any chance of escape?

"You going to introduce us, Kai?" Boone asked with a wolfish grin.

Kai. His name was Kai. Tessa's heart beat faster, as if she'd stumbled across some great secret and not just a name.

Kai. Kai. Kai. She cemented the lyrical sound into her mind while trying desperately to remember what Ella had said about him. But the man had such an effect on her, her brain couldn't quite kick into gear.

"Tessa Byrne," his deep voice resonated from behind her.

Tessa always thought of herself as forgettable, but this man had remembered her name after one brief mention in the dark. *He remembered,* she told herself, feeling a tiny glimmer of hope despite her desperate situation.

Hope that shattered the moment a third man grunted and spoke.

"Where did you find her, Kai?" he barked, still looming above her.

7

She wished she could see Kai, but no. And this new man — the leader, for sure — was staring at her so fiercely, she held her breath. His eyes sparked, and when she looked more closely, she could make out individual flames. Red, yellow, and orange, licking this way and that.

Silas. The head of the group. He had to be. Which meant he was a dragon like the man who'd attacked her.

Watch out for him, Ella had said. *He's a good man, but he's been through a lot, and he's testy.*

Testy? The guy was terrifying.

He doesn't trust humans, Ella had added. *Few dragons do.*

Tessa shrank back in the cushions. Shouldn't it be the other way around?

When a deep thrum sounded behind her, Silas tore his glare away from Tessa and aimed it at the man behind her.

That was Kai, she realized. Kai, growling in warning. Protecting her again.

"I didn't find her. She found us. And I think she can speak for herself," he rumbled.

If Tessa hadn't been so tense, she might have hugged him right there. But who was Kai, really? He'd stared at her all the way over from the garage — she'd felt his eyes on her back the whole time — and his nostrils had flared when he took in her scent. What kind of shifter did that? Ella had mentioned a tiger...

Tessa decided the man hanging back in the shadows, pacing back and forth at the perimeter of the open-walled space was the tiger.

Cruz. Stay out of his way if he's had a bad day, Ella had warned.

At the time, Tessa had wanted to say, *I'm the one having a bad day.* But now, she kept her lips sealed. Just in case.

So Kai wasn't the tiger. Tessa peered around. The big, burly guy standing two steps behind Silas was all ears and didn't say much. He could go from ferocious to friendly with the slightest twitch of his heavy eyebrows, and he tilted his head when the others spoke.

Hunter, the bear. All muscle. All loyalty. But a lot of pain.

Tessa let her gaze linger on Hunter just long enough to wonder where the pain came from. But then Kai stepped back into view, and all she could look at was him.

Kai wasn't bigger, taller, or more handsome than the others, but he took her breath away. Her pulse skipped, and she found herself leaning forward. What kind of shifter was he?

A not-to-be-fucked-with one, for sure. He bounded right up to Silas and put a hand on the man's broad chest in warning. Every man in the room tensed, and Tessa did, too. The two glared at each other with the force of two hurricanes about to collide.

Boone, the wolf shifter, murmured something too low for her to catch, trying to calm the two down. The bear lifted his boulder-sized shoulders and stepped closer, ready to break up a fight. The tiger's whiskers — er, two-day beard — twitched, and Tessa swore the air crackled with sheer power.

"Uh, guys," she said without thinking.

Every face whipped around in surprise, and the tension went back down a notch. But when she met Kai's eyes, her own inner storm field whirled into high gear. Her face flushed. Her blood pounded in her veins, and visions of thunderclouds raced through her mind along with the sound of whipping wind. Why did she have such a reaction to him?

Then his eyes sparked the way Silas's had, and Tessa froze.

Kai, another dragon, Ella's voice sounded in her mind. *Related to Silas. Every bit as dangerous but slightly more sane.*

She stared. Dragons. Holy shit. She'd been attacked by a dragon less than twenty-four hours ago. Why on earth had Ella said she would be safe here? Maybe Ella was part of some conspiracy. Maybe Ella wasn't to be trusted. Maybe—

"Who sent you here?" Silas demanded. "How did you find this place?"

"Ella sent me," Tessa said, feeling sick.

The tiger stopped pacing abruptly, and every man fell silent. Silas's eyebrows shot up. Kai nodded at her to go on.

They are good men, Ella had assured her. *Honorable men, if a little rough around the edges. They've been through so much, survived terrible things. You can trust them.*

Tessa blanched. How could she trust any of these men, least of all Kai? Dragons were the enemy, for goodness' sake!

Chapter Two

The woman's voice shook while she spoke, but her eyes were fierce, making Kai's inner dragon hum with pride. His whole body hummed, and he burned with the urge to step closer. To protect her. To touch her. To show her he cared.

But he didn't dare. Not with the other men around. Not with her shooting daggers at him.

She is strong. She is fierce, his inner dragon purred in approval.

She's human, he told his inner beast.

She is our mate, his dragon rumbled.

She couldn't be. She couldn't!

But damn it, even before he'd seen Tessa, he'd *felt* her presence, the way he had sensed all the important moments in his life half a second before they actually hit. It was as if destiny had tapped on his thick skull and said, *Watch out, mister. Here comes a moment you will never forget.*

He'd felt it the day his mother died, and the morning before he'd first been introduced to the men who would become brothers to him. The feeling didn't strike often — only on the couple of really momentous occasions of his life. And the premonition had certainly never struck him around a woman.

Until now.

He stared at her. Well, continued to stare was more like it, because he'd been captivated by Tessa from the start. Even in the moonlight, he'd marveled at her thick red hair. He'd been entranced by her clear, bright voice, even when it was tinged with fear. Her green eyes cast a spell on him, but shit — they were darting around the room, searching for a way out instead of dancing over him as they had before.

His dragon groaned and lashed its tail. *She trusted us at first. Now you've gone and frightened her.*

It wasn't his fault, damn it. Silas was the one looming over Tessa.

Then why is she staring at us like that? his dragon demanded.

"How do you know Ella?" Boone asked softly.

Kai tilted his head at the wolf, grateful for his calm, steady presence. Boone had been like that from the start — a lot like Hunter, the bear. They'd all joined separate branches of the military before chance — or destiny — threw the five of them together in an elite Special Forces unit. Their human commanders never suspected they were shifters, and they had been careful never to let on. Together, they had gone from ragtag group to hardened soldiers. Now, they were civilians again, trying to find their way in the world. Silas was the mastermind of their little gang. Kai had the sheer power, while Boone and Hunter were the glue that kept them together. Cruz was their heart, even if he liked to pretend he didn't care.

Kai glanced at Silas, dipping his chin slightly to his older cousin. All they had was each other, even if that was hard to remember when their inner dragons clashed.

And damn, was his dragon edgy tonight. Usually, Silas was the unpredictable one. But ever since Kai had brought Tessa in, his inner dragon had raged and screamed, demanding the others stay away.

Tessa gulped and raised her chin, afraid yet defiant. "Ella lives in the apartment next to mine. She came just in time to rescue me—"

"Rescue? From whom?" Silas demanded.

Kai's inner dragon roared at the thought of anyone threatening Tessa.

"Damien Morgan. A real estate tycoon from Phoenix, Arizona who. . ."

Silas's eyes shot to Kai's as Tessa trailed off at the sudden silence in the room.

Kai gave Silas a slight nod. *Yep. Damien fucking Morgan.* Kai itched to let his claws out.

"You know him?" Tessa asked. Then she frowned and murmured to herself. "Of course, you know him. He's a dragon, too."

Silas glared and barked without warning, making Tessa shrink back. "We are nothing like Damien. Nothing."

A sentiment Kai wholly agreed with, though he shoved Silas back and shot a warning into his cousin's mind. *Quit scaring her.*

You're both scaring her, Boone pointed out. *How about sitting down?*

Kai looked at his shoes, then took a deep breath and sat down on the couch — not too far, not too near Tessa, spreading his arms so no one else would dare intrude on her space.

"How do you know Damien Morgan?"

Tessa looked so downcast, he wanted to cuddle up beside her and hug the feeling right out of her. But fat chance of that if she thought all dragons were like Damien.

"I'm a private chef," she said, making Hunter's ears flick. Typical bear, obsessed with food. "He contracted me to cook for him, and I went to his new estate yesterday."

Kai huffed, picturing the place. He'd never been there, but he'd seen the pictures. They'd been on the cover of every architectural magazine because everything Damien did, he did big. That eagle's nest of his — the latest in a series of exclusive properties Damien owned around the world — appeared to have been half carved into the cliffside of Camelback Mountain in Phoenix. All glass and stone, with a flowing infinity pool, it was the perfect dragon's lair. According to the shifter grapevine, behind the mansion was a cave filled with unspeakable treasures. Treasures Damien had stolen from Kai's family not too long ago.

Kai growled, and Silas did, too.

Tessa trailed off, so Kai prompted her gently. "You went to his estate, and...?"

"His housekeeper let me in, and I didn't think I'd even meet him. But then he came in the kitchen, and he had this look on his face." Tessa's eyes grew wary and faraway. Her fingers fiddled with the pendant around her neck. "He came

ANNA LOWE

closer and closer, and then he sniffed me..." She trailed off, hunching her shoulders as if Damien were right there, trying to breathe her scent. "Then he backed me up and started saying all these crazy things. That I was his. That he had to have me. That—"

She stopped and shook her head, unwilling to share the rest. Kai didn't want to hear more anyway. He wanted to leap into the air, fly all the way to the mainland, and burn that bastard to a crisp. His breath heated just at the thought of it.

Silas shot him a look, crumpling his nose at the slight whiff of sulfur that accompanied a dragon's anger.

Sure, go ahead and breathe fire, Boone said. *That will really help her relax.*

Kai sucked in his lips and held his tongue.

Tessa took a deep breath and skipped something in her story. That much, Kai was sure of. "He started choking me, and I thought he was going to kill me..."

Not kill you, Kai almost said. *Just bring you to the edge, and then bring you back.* A sick form of foreplay some of his twisted brethren enjoyed before raping their victims. Some women were eventually released, so damaged they could scarcely recall what had happened. Others died before the "fun" ended, and their bodies were dumped somewhere far, far away.

He balled his fists, letting his nails dig into his palms. He and Silas never engaged in that cruel form of pleasure, but some individuals of their species did.

I'm killing Damien. I swear I will kill him, he told Silas.

Silas rolled his eyes. *Get in line, man. Get in line.*

"But then someone came to the door," Tessa went on, hugging herself. "Damien locked me in a room while he went to meet whoever it was, and I couldn't escape. But Ella came along and helped me out."

Silas nodded, and Boone grinned. *Good old Ella.*

Kai made a mental note to thank Ella when he got the chance. But the shifter was a desert fox, which made her impossible to pin down. She'd served in the military beside Kai and the others in their secret, elite corps.

"How do you know Ella?" Silas asked. "And how do you know about shifters?"

Tessa made a face. "I didn't until yesterday. But I was so freaked out after I saw Damien's fangs, I made Ella explain."

Cruz, the tiger, growled his thoughts into everyone's mind. *Coincidence that Ella was living next door to her? That Ella came along at exactly the right time to save this woman from Damien?*

No coincidence, Silas agreed. *Ella had to have been watching Tessa — or Damien. She hates him as much as we do.*

But why would Morgan be after this woman? Why would he be interested in a human? Boone asked.

Kai bit back a growl. How could anyone *not* be interested in Tessa? Even before he saw her at the gate to the property, he'd felt her pull on him like a magnet. He'd rushed home early from town just to satisfy the instinct that something terribly important demanded his attention — immediately. And there she'd been, standing at the gate.

Told you, his dragon nodded. *She's ours. Destiny brought her here.*

He didn't want to believe it, but it sure as hell didn't seem like the other guys were as entranced by her beauty, her scent, her... her everything.

"I wanted to go to the police, but Ella told me they'd never believe me. She said to come here. To ask you for help." Tessa's eyes shone, and she blinked back tears. Tears of sorrow? Fear?

Tears of pride, his dragon murmured. *Our mate is strong.*

"So I caught the first flight and—"

Silas threw his hands up. "You booked a flight? Using a credit card?"

She shook her head. "I don't think he can trace me."

"Damien Morgan can trace anyone anywhere." Silas frowned.

Tessa shook her head again, and Kai's heart swelled. Few people dared contradict Silas, but Tessa didn't seem cowed. Not even by a dragon.

"I don't think so. My clients know me as Thérèse Brûler."
She shrugged. "When I just started out in the business, it was
hard to find work, and a friend suggested a catchier name."

"Did it work?" Boone asked, flashing his wolf's grin.

Tessa managed a little smile, and Kai wished it was him
who'd done that to her.

Someday, we will, his dragon vowed. *We will make her so
happy, she'll smile at us every day.*

"It did." Tessa lit up for a second before her face fell. "But
look where that got me."

"You didn't know about Damien," Kai said.

She'd been avoiding his eyes, but now she met his gaze
again, a little less frightened than before. Did she understand
that there were good dragons and bad dragons just as there
were good and bad humans?

"I guess I didn't." She looked around the room and sucked
in a deep breath. "I didn't know about any kind of shifters."

"Well, don't let dragons give all of us a bad name," Boone
wisecracked. "Like I said, we don't bite."

"Not even wolves?" Tessa shot back.

Boone grinned. "Wolves are very civilized. But don't get
me started on tigers."

In the corner of the room, Cruz let out a low, feline growl.

Tessa laughed. She actually laughed.

*Either she's the world's toughest human, or she's so ex-
hausted she can't see straight,* Hunter observed in his low, griz-
zly voice.

Kai nudged the glass of water closer. Hunter was right.
Tessa's green eyes had dark circles beneath them, and her face
looked pinched. And after what she'd been through. . .

Tessa slumped. "I didn't know what else to do. I didn't
know where to go."

"We'll help you," Kai said immediately. "You can stay
here."

Boone coughed. Silas elbowed him in the gut, and Cruz
snarled, pushing his protest into his fellow shifter's minds.

She can't stay here. No humans. We agreed.

Kai whirled to glare at the tiger.

16

I thought you distrusted humans as much as I do, Cruz's yellow-tinted tiger eyes met his.

Kai caught the words, *I do,* on his tongue.

His dragon shrugged. *We do distrust humans. Just not this one.*

Silas shot him a sidelong glance. *Why are you so bent on protecting this human?*

It didn't seem prudent to blurt, *Because I think she's my mate,* so he just growled. *A dragon threatened her. It's our duty to set this straight.*

Silas considered and finally nodded to Tessa. "It's late. We have a guesthouse where you can stay — for now." He gave Kai a pointed stare then softened when he turned back to Tessa. "You'll be safe here. I give you my word. You'll be safe."

Tessa clutched at the fabric of the couch, and her fingers played over her necklace as she wavered. The stone pendant was a deep, rich green, exactly the color of her eyes.

Kai looked at her, begging for her attention, and she finally glanced his way.

You'll be safe here, he promised, communicating with his eyes. His body. His soul. *I give you my word, you'll be safe.*

The longer he looked into those incredible green eyes, the more time seemed to slow down. The room blurred away, as did the other men, and all sound muted but for the beating of his heart.

Mate, his dragon whispered. *This is our mate.*

He wanted to will the words into her mind, but she was human. How could she possibly hear? How could she understand about the eternal bond that united two shifters?

"Tessa," Silas hissed, and *bang* — Kai snapped back to the world. Tessa blinked as if she, too, had drifted away.

"Yes. I mean, thank you," she said, suddenly flustered. "I mean..."

Silas nodded wearily. "Boone, show her the way."

Kai almost leaped to block the wolf, but Silas threw an arm in his way. *You stay here. We need to talk.*

"Right this way," Boone said, leading Tessa out into the night.

She balked, looking at Kai, whose soul cried. He wanted to be the one to show her the way, to keep her safe. But Silas's grip on his shirt was tight, and the look on his face said he meant business, so Kai turned to Tessa and promised her all over again. He nearly drifted off into that hypnotized, *can't drag my eyes off hers* state again, too.

"Kai." Silas yanked on his sleeve.

"Come on, Tessa," Boone said at exactly the same time.

She looked at him once more, then stepped out into the night and slipped into the shadows with Boone.

Kai's dragon roared inside. *Not Boone! He can't have her! He—*

Kai did his best to ignore the voice. Boone was a good man he'd trust with his life.

Do you trust him with our mate? his dragon cried.

Kai gritted his teeth and turned slowly back to Silas. Hunter and Cruz slunk into the night, too, leaving Kai and his cousin alone. To fight? To talk? Kai wondered which it would be.

Silas paced behind the bar and poured himself a brandy. He didn't offer Kai any. He just lifted the glass and pointed an accusing finger.

"Let me repeat the question. Why are you so interested in this human?"

Kai gnashed his teeth. How could he answer when he wasn't entirely sure himself? So he lied. "Like I said. Another dragon threatened her. It's our duty to set this straight."

Silas glared, but the anger, Kai knew, wasn't aimed at him. "Goddamn Damien Morgan. And if he's still working for Drax..."

Kai froze as a cold, icy feeling tiptoed down his back. "Drax?"

Silas nodded and said it louder as if to prove he wasn't afraid of the name. "Drax."

"Are you sure?"

"I can't be sure of anything when it comes to those bastards."

Silas's eyes flared, and Kai wondered again what had happened in the past. Silas was only older by a few years, but he'd left home much earlier than Kai. He'd come home scarred and tight-lipped. A short time later, he'd joined the army. When Kai's guardian died, Kai had followed Silas into the service, not knowing what else to do. That was a good ten years ago, and now... He shook his head at himself. Now he was scarred and tight-lipped, too.

He glanced in the direction Tessa had gone, wondering at all the feelings she'd stirred up. Things he hadn't felt for a long, long time.

He thumped his fist on the counter, because letting out anger was more acceptable than showing anything that made him soft. "Fucking Damien Morgan."

They'd only crossed paths twice, but it was enough to convince Kai what an arrogant, selfish ass Morgan was. Some shifters hid from the human world entirely. Others did their best to fit in and even to serve, like Kai, Silas, and their brothers-in-arms had. A few, however, used their unique shifter abilities to consolidate power and wealth. Shifters like Damien Morgan, the real estate tycoon, and even worse, Drax, the most powerful dragon of all.

"Real estate tycoon, my ass," Kai muttered, thinking of the land Morgan had cheated his family out of when they were at their most vulnerable — two decades earlier, when the older generation died and the up-and-comers were too young to resist. He took the brandy from Silas and poured himself two fingers. "We should have taken him out a long time ago. Both of them — Morgan and Drax."

Silas let out a bitter chuckle. "I tried. Believe me, I tried." He rubbed his right arm, where his sleeve hid the scars.

Kai put the bottle down with a thump. "How much are we going to let them get away with?"

"We don't know if they're working together on this."

"But if they are?"

"I guess we'll find out soon enough. We have a day — maximum two — before Morgan figures out Tessa's real name and tracks her down."

Kai bristled, and his dragon nearly let out a puff of fire. *No one touches my mate.*

"Let him come," Kai said. "Let him fight."

Silas shook his head. "Morgan, we might be able to take on. But if Drax is involved... I want to take down Drax as much as anyone, but we're not ready yet. You know that."

"How much more ready can we be?"

"Drax has more men, a hell of a lot more money, and dozens of spies."

"We have spies, too," Kai noted.

Silas raised his glass in a salute. "Thank goodness for Ella."

Kai raised his glass, too. "To Ella, then."

"To Ella," Silas agreed, toasting the night.

"And to taking down Damien Morgan," Kai added. "The first chance we get."

Chapter Three

"Right this way," Boone said, gesturing ahead.

Tessa hung back a little. Was she really going to follow a werewolf into the night? She glanced up at the moon, then at Boone's broad back, and finally over her shoulder to the open-sided building they'd just left.

Kai. Something kept pulling her back to Kai. But, damn — he was a dragon, just like the one who'd attacked her.

Dragons are insanely possessive, Ella had warned her. *Once they see something they want, they never give up.*

Ella had been talking about Damien Morgan, of course, but surely that applied to Kai, too. Still, Tessa hesitated. Every instinct drew her toward Kai, just as every instinct had told her to keep away from Damien Morgan.

She forced one foot in front of the other and followed Boone, watching him closely. At that point, a werewolf seemed like the lesser of two evils — as long as he didn't start howling at the moon.

Boone caught her upward glance and chuckled. "Don't worry. The moon isn't what makes us shift."

Shift. She turned the word over in her head. He said it so casually, like any creature could transform from human to animal.

"What does make you shift, then?" she asked, following him warily down the footpath.

Boone ducked under a leaf the size of an umbrella and paused, holding it up for her to pass.

"We can control when we shift." That made her feel slightly better — until he added, "Well, most of the time."

"Most of the time?" She stopped in her tracks.

Boone just strode on like it was any other Sunday in Hawaii. But it wasn't. It was midnight of the day she'd had her world turned upside down.

"You're not so different, I bet," he said as the sound of waves breaking over a coral-strewn shore grew louder.

"I'm pretty sure I'm very different. I've never sprouted fur or fangs."

"I mean controlling it." He stopped and looked at the moon. "Like when you're mad. Most of the time, you control it, right? But every once in a while, something happens, and you snap." His voice grew hushed. Regretful, almost.

Tessa looked up, too, trying to find a star that might orient her to this new place. It was so unlike Arizona — so alive, so green. So full of noises, like the swish of leaves against each other and the whisper of water over the beach.

Yes, she knew a thing or two about losing her temper. As a child, she'd had uncontrollable outbursts.

She's fiery, like her hair, her mother used to say.

Fiery, like our ancestors, her grandmother would add, though her mother always scoffed at that.

"Every human has an animal side," Boone said quietly. "Being a shifter just brings it to the surface."

Tessa furrowed her brow. "Like Ella?"

"Desert fox." Boone grinned. "Cunning as anything. Great legs, too."

Tessa snorted, but Boone just laughed. "What can I say? I'm a wolf."

The trail wound on, and Tessa wondered how big the estate was.

"What about dragons?" she asked when her thoughts drifted back to Kai.

"What about them?"

"Does something suddenly make them snap, too?"

Boone stopped and turned, scratching his brow. "Look, I know what you're thinking..."

Tessa doubted that, because her mind kept flipping back to the moment she'd brushed shoulders with Kai. To the pop

22

of electricity that had zipped around her body. The rush of warmth. The feeling of security.

"You can trust Kai and Silas. They have their rough spots, but hell, we all do." He scratched his chest, looking rueful. "It's guys like Damien Morgan you need to watch out for."

Tessa laughed bitterly. "If only someone told me that before I went to his house."

Boone shrugged. "Anyway, I'm guessing you've had enough to digest for one night. Time to catch some rest."

He motioned ahead, and she followed in spite of herself. The foliage thinned gradually, and the sound of the sea grew louder, drawing her on. Then Boone turned a corner and—

"Wow," she breathed when they stepped into the open.

A row of palms stood like so many flagpoles along the beach, their fronds swaying in the night breeze. Moonlight glittered over the ocean — not just in little glimpses but in a long, silver line drawn straight across the sea. The moonlight sparkled and danced over the water, casting everything in an indigo light.

"Beautiful," she breathed.

"Welcome to Hawaii." Boone grinned. "Now get some rest."

He waved to the right, and her jaw dropped. "That's the guesthouse?"

"Yep."

"And I get to stay there?"

He laughed. "All yours."

She took a step forward, then stopped again, staring at a vision from a travel magazine. The beach bungalow was tiny, but perfect. It started right where the beach ended, with a small step up to a low porch. A banana-colored kayak was pulled up beside the porch, inviting her to switch her inner clock to island time. The long, curved roof of palm fronds swept high in the middle and down at each end, sheltering a deep porch with two lounge chairs. The entire structure screamed *time to relax.*

Boone rolled a sliding door aside. His height made the place look even smaller and cozier.

"It's like a hobbit hole with a thatched roof," Tessa exclaimed.

He laughed and flicked the light switch, revealing a blue-and-yellow interior that soothed her nerves. "Don't tell Silas that."

She didn't have the energy to wonder what he meant.

"Good night," Boone murmured, turning back down the path.

"Wait — what about tomorrow?" she cried, gripping the doorframe.

He shrugged. "What about it?"

"I mean, what happens next?"

He tilted his head left and right. "I'm a wolf, not a soothsayer. But don't worry. Everything will be all right."

How did he know that? How could he be so sure?

"*Aloha po.* Good night," Boone said and disappeared down the path.

Tessa hugged herself and gazed out over the sea. Was she really going to spend the night among perfect strangers who turned into wild beasts?

Did she have a choice?

Briefly, she considered the kayak. No one would notice if she hopped in and paddled away. She could make her way to someplace down the coast, hitch a ride back to town, check herself in to a hotel, and figure out what to do next.

The moonlight winked off the sea, reminding her of the real problem. Morgan. The evil dragon was out there, and if he was searching for her. . .

She backed away from the kayak, studying the shadows. Maybe staying was her best bet. If she left now, she might walk right into her true enemy.

A bauble hung in a window, glinting blue in the moonlight — a pure, clean blue, just like Kai's eyes.

If you leave now, it seemed to say, *you'll never discover the mystery behind those amazing eyes, either.*

Her whole soul warmed, and her cheeks flushed as if Kai were actually there asking for a goodnight kiss. A kiss her soul yearned for, even if her mind resisted.

He's a dragon. He's dangerous, just like Morgan, who thinks he can take what he wants.

He's nothing like Morgan, a little voice in the back of her mind protested. *You can trust him. You should trust him.*

She took a deep breath, undecided. Then she checked the sky — no sign of dragons, thank goodness — and hurried inside, just in case.

Chapter Four

To her utter surprise, Tessa slept soundly from the moment she lay her head on the soft pillow of her queen-size bed to... to whatever time the scratch of a palm over the roof woke her up. She lay blinking at the thatched roof, amazed she'd slept free of nightmares. A few dreams had drifted through her mind, but they were all vague and blurry. She'd felt warm, relaxed, and protected, like a winter wanderer who'd stumbled into a cabin with a crackling fireplace. In place of winter, though, there'd been a tropical wonderland, and instead of being curled up in front of a fireplace, she'd been snuggled up in the nook of something leathery and safe. Something with a gentle curve to it, like a crescent-shaped couch.

Daylight bathed the bungalow, doing its best to creep in under the low edge of the roof. For a moment, it even felt as if Boone had spoken the truth — that everything would be all right.

But when Tessa studied her dreams more closely, her heart started pounding again. That wasn't a couch she'd imagined nestling against. It was a slumbering dragon who'd kept his wing looped over her, forming a shelter.

She jumped out the bed and threw the front door open, suddenly desperate for fresh air.

The sun sparkled off the sea much as the moonlight had, and a shearwater flew past. *Nothing to worry about,* its graceful arc through the air seemed to say. *Nothing to worry about here.*

Tessa eyed the thick vegetation all around. Nothing to worry about? What if a tiger came wandering out of the underbrush with bloody prey in its mouth? Or if a bear came lumbering down the path, nose to the breeze? She glanced upward. A dragon could swoop overhead at any moment, throwing her world into shadow again.

She retreated into the little bungalow, wondering what to do.

Routine, her grandmother used to tell her each time she had to shuttle between her parents' homes. One week here, another week there. *The most important thing is to maintain your routine. Then you'll feel at home no matter where you are.*

She doubted she'd ever feel at home in a place surrounded by shifters. But then again, she didn't have to stay long. Just long enough to figure out how to evade Damien Morgan and get back to living her life.

There was instant coffee in the tiny kitchenette, and a shower off to the side with nice, fluffy towels rolled into tidy rows. Tessa touched them, then glanced around the neat-as-a-pin bungalow. Who did the housekeeping on this estate? More shifters? Humans? Fairies?

She pushed the thought out of her mind and concentrated on one thing at a time, starting with a shower. The airline had lost the luggage she'd packed in her hasty departure from Arizona, so she'd slept in her top and underwear. A quick perusal of the closet turned up a selection of plain T-shirts in various sizes, as well as sarongs, so at least there was that — not to mention a toothbrush by the sink, thank God.

The shower made her feel fresher and stronger, but the coffee only made her hungrier, so she gathered her nerves and stepped outside.

Koa Point, Ella had said. *Koa means an elite class of warrior.*

Tessa turned in a slow circle. The warrior part fit, for sure, but Koa might as well have meant *heavenly place where the land meets the sea,* judging by the breathtaking view.

She wandered slowly up the path Boone had brought her down the previous night. Trails branched off in every direction, and a corrugated roof showed to the right. There seemed to be a number of houses tucked away in their own private corners of the estate, and she wondered who lived where. Most of all, she wondered where Kai lived. Did all dragons live in high perches, like Damien Morgan? The estate extended from the seashore to... Well, she couldn't tell how far. The property was plenty big, that was for sure.

The foliage opened briefly, and she glimpsed a helipad where a brown helicopter with yellow and red stripes stood on a square patch of cement. She pursed her lips and walked on. Whoever owned the estate really had it all.

When she came out on a lawn by the open-sided building where she'd met the men the previous night, her steps slowed, and she adjusted the sarong around her waist. She wished she had a mirror — not to mention a can of Mace. Could she trust these men? Couldn't she?

Slowly, she approached, eyeing the space. Was anyone there?

The thatched building was as simple as they came — just a concrete floor carpeted with woven mats and some supports for the roof — yet elegant at the same time. The burgundy couch she'd used the previous night was one of four set in a square in what made up the living room portion of the space. The clock standing on the table said eleven.

Whoa — eleven? She did a double take. Had she really slept that long?

"Morning," a deep voice rumbled from her left.

She turned and saw Hunter sitting at the kitchen counter. His hair was mussed and his eyes sleepy as he stirred a bowl of porridge.

"Morning," she managed, trying not to sound too surprised. Were bears late risers or had he had a late night?

He smiled, stirred a dollop of honey into his oatmeal, and sighed at the first bite.

Tessa decided she could deal with the bear. The wolf had been friendly enough, too, but what about the others? The tiger was there, too, but the moment he saw her, he picked up his plate and left.

"Never mind Cruz," Kai's smooth voice said.

She whirled and found him standing at the far side of the shelter, leaning against the twisted wooden trunk that formed

29

ANNA LOWE

one of the ceiling supports.

Even in daylight, the man was all angles and shadowy shapes. His cheekbones were high and chiseled. His eyebrows curved up. The black T-shirt he wore stretched across a hell of a lot of chest, and his fingers gripped the natural wood column so hard his knuckles were white. Which was funny because she was the nervous one, right?

"I don't think Cruz likes me," she managed, ripping her gaze away from Kai. Telling her heart there was absolutely no reason for it to go pitter-pat.

"Don't take it personally," Boone said, coming up behind Kai. "He doesn't like any humans."

The wolf was every bit as tall and chiseled as Kai, but it was the dragon who commanded her attention. She couldn't drag her eyes or mind away from him. Then it struck her. Did Kai like humans?

Silas appeared from along the path, nodding a greeting, and she wondered the same thing. Did Silas hate her? Resent her? Did he simply want her to go away?

"Hungry?" Kai asked.

The second her eyes bounced back over to him, her mind came up with a dozen possible interpretations of *hungry.*

"Help yourself," Boone said, motioning toward the kitchen. He pulled the freezer door open, took out a frozen pizza, and popped it in the stove.

Tessa came around and peeked in the fridge. The shelves were packed with condiments and appetizers, but nothing approaching a proper meal. There were pickles, five kinds of mustard, three kinds of milk — one of which looked long past its expiration date — and a forlorn lump of cheese. No fresh fruit or vegetables other than half a pineapple turned upside down on a plate. Maybe the estate really was one big bachelor pad. She peeked into the garbage, and sure enough — it was filled with takeout containers.

"Find something?" Kai asked, coming up behind her. Close, but not close enough for her taste.

Found you, she wanted to say.

30

She forced in a slow, steadying breath. Why did he make her blood heat?

"Um. . . well. . ."

He crooked an eyebrow at her, a look that was part James Dean, part 1960s Clint Eastwood. She knew because she'd had black-and-white images of both on the wall of her college dorm room, way back when.

"This will be fine." She straightened quickly, pulling out the cheese.

"Someone has to go shopping," the bear said, looking at the others. "There's not much left. Who's cooking tonight, anyway?"

The room went still. Silas looked at Kai. Kai looked at Boone. Boone looked at Hunter, whose eyes hit the floor.

"Didn't you say you were a private chef?" Boone said, and four pairs of hungry shifter eyes turned to Tessa.

She nodded, shifting her weight from foot to foot. Being the center of attention didn't bother her, but the men were so. . . intense. So powerful. So. . . larger than life.

"Perfect. I nominate the human." Boone grinned. "To make dinner, I mean. Not to be dinner."

Tessa put her hands on her hips. "Very funny."

A growl sounded, and she saw Kai shooting Boone a withering look.

"Sure," she said, projecting calm before those two worked themselves into a glaring contest. "I'd love to make dinner."

"You don't have to," Silas said, none too pleased.

"It's the least I can do. How far is the grocery store? Can anyone take me?"

Boone started to raise his hand, but he glanced at Kai and immediately dropped it again.

"I'll take you," Kai said firmly.

Just what she'd been hoping for — and against. Something about him terrified her at the same time that it titillated. Her heart thumped wildly, and her face flushed.

"Great," she said, trying to sound casual. "What would everyone like?"

"Steak," they all grunted at the same time.

Tessa nearly took a step back. Okay, so steak it was. "Rare, or do I have to ask?"

"Rare." Boone nodded.

"Definitely rare," Kai agreed.

"Rare with honey glazing," Hunter murmured.

Tessa looked around. If she could win these shifters' hearts through their stomachs, so be it.

"We need to talk first," Silas said, as dark and intent as ever.

And just like that, reality came crashing back in. These weren't new clients she could enjoy cooking for. They were shifters who were every bit as dangerous as Damien Morgan. Maybe even more dangerous. There were five of them, after all.

Then again, if they'd wanted to kill, rape, or torture her, they would have already done so.

"Sure," she said, hating that her voice wavered. "We can talk."

Silas tilted his head, leading her past the couches to a table in the corner where he pulled a chair out for her, ever the gentleman. But before she could sit, Kai squeezed between the two of them and grabbed the chair.

No one seats this woman but me, his stiff back said.

Tessa looked at Silas, then at Kai, and found them glaring at each other in a replay of the previous night's showdown.

"Maybe I'll just sit here," she murmured, maneuvering around to another spot.

Behind her, Boone chuckled then shut up the moment the dragons glared at him.

Tessa shook her head. Shifters. How was she ever going to make sense of them?

Silas seemed to have the manners of an era long gone. Boone, on the other hand, was a modern, feet-up-on-the-coffee-table kind of guy. Kai was somewhere in between. Were they just different personalities, or did every species have its own unique characteristics?

Kai took the seat next to her, leaving the chair across the table for Silas. Having Kai close settled her fluttery nerves, but his attentiveness scared her, too.

Dragons are insanely possessive, Ella had said. *Once they see something they want, they never give up.*

She sat down and knotted her hands on the table, telling herself this would be just like the police report she would have filed if she'd been attacked by a human and not a shifter.

No one can know about shifters. No one. You understand? Ella had taken her by both arms to impress the point, whispering in a corner of the airport as they waited for Tessa's flight.

"Tell us from the beginning," Silas said, taking a seat opposite her and Kai.

Her nervous hands went straight to the pendant around her neck. Silas's eyes shone with interest, and she quickly tucked the emerald look-alike under her shirt. Was it true about dragons and treasure? If so, couldn't they tell it was a worthless fake? Worthless, that is, except for the sentimental value it held.

"Damien Morgan's assistant phoned me," she said quickly. "He said Morgan was trying out different chefs for the few occasions he spent in town, and we spent forever making an appointment."

He's a very busy man, the assistant had said in a haughty voice.

"Busy where?" Silas cut in.

Silas wanted to know everything: the extent of Morgan's business interests, his contacts, his daily routine — the kind of details any police detective would ask. But Tessa barely knew Morgan enough to answer.

"That was my first time at his house." *First and last time,* she thought to herself.

"And he attacked you out of nowhere?"

She considered. "One second, he was sniffing the onion soup, and the next, he was sniffing me." She shivered. "Then he grabbed me and pinned me against the wall." She hunched over, unwilling to relive the terror of it all. The skin-crawling weirdness, too, when Morgan crowed something about mates and breeding and—

She fast-forwarded through that part. "Then the doorbell rang, and he shoved me into another room."

"And Ella showed up out of nowhere?"

Tessa nodded. "That was the strange part. It was as if she'd followed me up there in case something happened. Wait." Her blood ran cold. "Do you think Ella had something to do with—"

Silas cut her off immediately. "You can trust Ella."

"Are you sure?" Tessa had been so grateful for Ella's help that she hadn't stopped to think about it much. But in retrospect, it seemed strange that the woman from the apartment next to hers would save her from a dragon. It was as if Ella had suspected something was afoot. But what?

"We're sure," Silas said so firmly, she didn't dare question him. "What we don't understand is why Morgan targeted you."

Target. Tessa hated the sound of that. But it was the truth.

"Do you think he'll try to find me?"

Silas tipped his head this way and that. "Depends. Did he show his dragon?"

Tessa gripped the edge of the table and closed her eyes. "His fingernails turned into claws, and his ears extended." She swept her fingers over her own ears as if to mold the corners upward, Spock-style. "His eyes glowed red like lava. Like a fire. Like... like..." She struggled for the word momentarily, then pointed at Silas. "Like yours."

She trembled at the sight of sparks and flicks of flame in Silas's eyes but forced herself not to flinch. Maybe dragons were like dogs or horses — creatures a person shouldn't show their fear to.

She glanced at Kai just to prove how tough she was — even if she was a mess inside — and froze. His eyes were glowing, too, but there was blue mixed in with the orange and red. A rich, pure blue, like the innermost part of a fire. More beautiful than frightening.

Silas made a harsh, clearing-his-throat sound that had to be some kind of signal. Kai blinked, dousing the blue flame. Tessa turned away hastily, studying her hands. What was that about? Was there a color code to dragon eyes? If so, what the heck did blue mean?

"Nothing else?" Silas demanded. "Did he show his teeth? His wings? His tail?"

Tessa chortled. "I'm pretty sure I would have died on the spot if he showed me his teeth. Well, his canines extended a little."

"Like this?" Silas opened his mouth, curling back his lips and—

Tessa threw up her hands. "Please don't demonstrate. I'm not ready for that yet." So not ready.

"What else did you see?" Kai asked.

"I looked through the keyhole and saw another man come in. I couldn't see his face, but I did see Morgan, and his arms turned into wings as he paced back and forth. Thank God Ella tapped on the window and helped me escape."

Ella, who'd coaxed her along an inch-wide railing over a sheer cliff, then shifted to fox form and guided Tessa down the steep slope, away from that awful place.

Tessa closed her eyes and held her pendant tightly, fighting back the taste of bile. To think how close she'd come to a horrible fate...

"Tessa," Kai whispered. Well, she thought it was Kai, though she'd never imagined his voice could be so soft or so kind.

She looked up.

"Not all dragons are evil, Tessa. Damien Morgan is an exception."

His eyes pleaded with her — really pleaded, as if it was incredibly important to him that she understood. His eyes glowed again, and he seemed to hold his breath.

Her cheeks warmed, and the rest of the room faded slowly away until it was just her, Kai, and the promise in his eyes. The plea.

Please trust me. Know that I will never hurt you. Never, his eyes said. Dragon eyes just like the ones in her dream. *I will protect you to the end of my days.*

For one magical moment, all the anxiety eased out of her soul, and she wished she had her own glowing-eyes trick. One that could tell him, *I believe you. I trust you.*

She might even have been bewitched enough to add something crazy like, *I think I could even love you,* if Silas hadn't thumped his mug on the table and broken the spell.

"What did Morgan say? Tell me his exact words."

She hugged herself and leaned back as Morgan's words flooded through her mind, drowning away Kai's.

You will make me a good mate, he'd said, exhaling a sulfurous breath in her face. *You will breed me many heirs, and I will become the most powerful of my kind.*

"I don't remember," she whispered, hoping dragons couldn't smell a lie.

Chapter Five

Kai could see Tessa wearing down under the questions, and it nearly killed him to see her relive the horror of what had happened.

Give her a break, already, he barked at Silas.

They were getting nowhere, and Tessa was growing more and more distraught. Not that she showed it — much. The brave little human was doing her best to put on a soldier's face. But still, the strain showed. A few minutes earlier, she had cracked the dawn of a smile — back when the topic was dinner, that is. Now that they were discussing her near-death at the hands of the dragon he hated more than any other on earth, she was white as a sheet.

Silas was unrelenting, as Kai normally would be, but enough was enough. He allowed Silas two more questions before pushing his chair back and announcing, "We need to go before the stores close."

Silas furrowed his brow. The stores were nowhere near closing, and they both knew it.

Enough with the questions, he told Silas. *Let me see what I can get out of her on the drive into town.*

"Maybe we can check on my luggage, too," Tessa said, sounding so exhausted, Kai nearly took her hand.

"Not sure it's a good idea for you to leave the estate." Silas stood quickly, blocking the way.

Kai drilled Silas with his hardest glare. *She'll be with me.*

Silas gave him one of those *That's what I'm worried about* looks he excelled at.

Look, she's barely over the shock, Kai said. *It's just as much of a puzzle to her as to us. Let's give her a little time. She might remember an important detail if she feels more in her element.*

Silas's fiery eyes darted from Kai to Tessa and back. Finally, he gave a slow nod. "Just be careful."

The second Kai stood and took Tessa's hand, he knew what Silas meant about being careful. Just that bit of contact with the human made his dragon come alive.

Mine! My mate!

Yeah, he had to be careful, all right — with his heart.

Not keeping her, he scolded his dragon. *Just helping her for now.*

Forever, his dragon huffed.

"Maybe you can reach Ella in the meantime," Kai told Silas, trying to distract his dragon.

"Been trying all morning," Silas sighed, watching them go. Kai could tell from the burning feeling in his back.

Watch what you let yourself feel for that human, Silas murmured into his mind. *Watch out.*

Kai hurried Tessa around the corner toward the garage.

"Um, Kai?"

He played her voice back in his mind, exulting in the sound of his name on his tongue.

"Yes?"

"Do we have to go so fast?"

Oops. His steps had grown faster and faster until he was practically jogging along.

Her legs are long, but not that long, his dragon murmured. *Slow down.*

"Sorry," he murmured, forcing himself to a walk.

"Kai?" Tessa asked a second later, setting off the fireworks in him again.

"Yes?"

"You're crushing my hand."

Oops. He let go immediately but grabbed it again a second later, ordering himself not to squeeze this time. "Sorry. It's just that Silas can get to me at times. He's a little intense."

She snorted and gave him a pointed look. "*Silas* is a little intense?"

He glanced at her, and there it was again. That fire, that roar in her eyes. Little flicks of orange and red amidst the green.

She'd make a good dragon, his inner beast hummed.

He pursed his lips. *Bet Dad thought that about Mom.*

That shut his dragon up, and it brought back all the memories, too. Faint memories of the mother who'd died when he was young. A human mated to a dragon, she'd been unable to defend herself against a rogue dragon attack. Rogues who'd been tipped off by humans. His father had never forgiven himself, and he'd died not long after hunting down the rogues who killed his mate.

Is that what you want for Tessa? he barked.

His dragon side refused to reply, so he went on, hammering in his point.

That's why she can't be ours. Get that into your head. No humans. We can't put her in that kind of jeopardy.

She already is in jeopardy, his dragon pointed out. *It's us keeping her safe.*

Kai stomped along. If only it were that simple.

"Kai?"

Tessa's voice cut through the storm cloud of emotions spinning around his heart, settling him down again. "Yes?"

"You okay?"

Now it was her squeezing his hand hard. He grinned in spite of himself.

"Fine," he murmured. "Thanks."

They continued up the driveway in silence.

Quit staring at her, he ordered his dragon.

You try not staring at a woman that beautiful, the beast shot back.

He was trying, but yes — mostly failing. The white T-shirt brought out the brilliant green of her eyes, and the colorful sarong she'd matched it with was tied in some complicated way that emphasized the perfect curve of her hips. Her hair bounced over her shoulders, glinting reddish-gold in the sun. More girl-next-door pretty than cover-girl gorgeous with her freckles and thin lips, but damn. She had more soul than a

ANNA LOWE

dozen hollow-eyed cover models put together. More spunk. More spark. He could see it in her eyes and in her quick, bouncy step.

"Nice necklace," he said when she caught him looking her way yet again.

She caught the pendant and held it up for him. It looked a hell of a lot like an emerald — green exactly the color of her eyes. The stone's shape seemed familiar in a way Kai couldn't explain.

"It's not a real emerald, but my grandmother gave it to me, so it means a lot to me," she murmured. She smiled at the pendant — a bittersweet smile that made him yearn to find out more, though he didn't dare ask — and then she tucked it away again.

"So, dragons can fly, right?" she asked.

Of course, I can fly, his dragon snorted.

"Yes."

"So why all the cars?" she asked, waving her hand down the long, arched line of garages they'd finally reached.

"Oh. The owner of the estate collects them."

"I see," she said in a tone that indicated she didn't understand at all. "Who is the owner?"

He grabbed a key from a set of hooks and continued walking — past the Jaguar he'd driven the previous night. Past the Ferrari, the Lamborghini, and the Jeep. "It's complicated."

"Try me."

He hemmed and hawed because it wasn't entirely clear to him, either. Silas had left the military a few months before the rest of them had, and by the time Kai and the others joined him on Maui, Silas had sealed the caretaking deal and made it clear not to ask questions about the owner.

"It's a special deal. The owner is hardly ever here. We keep an eye on the place. Like caretakers."

"Caretakers?" She raised an eyebrow. "What exactly do you take care of?"

Kai waved a hand vaguely. "You know. The estate."

"Like what? Do you mow the lawns?"

He shook his head. Hell, no. The gardener did that.

40

"Fix plumbing?"

Well, no. But—

"Do you take care of all these cars?"

That, he had an answer for. "Hunter does. He's the mechanic."

"So, what do you do?"

There she went, turning the tables on him, asking a million questions.

"What are you — a private investigator?" he joked.

"No. Are you?"

He opened his mouth then closed it again, not quite sure whether to admit the truth.

"You're kidding," Tessa said.

He shook his head.

"Prove it."

Now he remembered why Cruz disliked humans so much. Always prying. Though the way Tessa did it was so. . . cute.

"Prove it," she insisted.

He sighed, drew out his wallet, and showed her his ID.

Tessa, of course, pulled it right out of his hands and inspected it closely. "Pilot's license? Dragons need pilot's licenses?"

"Oops. That's for the helicopter," he said, turning his wallet around in her hands and flipping to the next card.

"The helicopter. Of course," she muttered then caught herself. "Whoa, wait. Why would a dragon need a helicopter?"

He shrugged. "Business."

She didn't seem convinced. "Do all the guys here have pilot's licenses?"

Kai laughed outright. "Nah. Boone doesn't mind flying, but try getting a bear or a tiger in a helicopter. The big boys get all white-knuckled."

Tessa gaped as she read his next ID card. "State of Hawaii. . ." She trailed off and whistled. "You're really a private eye?"

"You're a private chef," he tried, motioning her into the Land Rover with tinted windows.

"Minor difference," she said, climbing in.

He eased the vehicle down the road, keeping his eyes ahead.

"You can actually make a living as a private eye?"

"Can you actually make a living as a private chef?"

"Yep," she said with a note of pride. "It's a good business once you make a name for yourself." She frowned. "Except for dragons, of course."

"Not all dragons are bad," he said.

She looked at him for a long, hard minute, clearly undecided. But she'd gotten in the car with him, right?

"Quit changing the subject," she said. "Tell me what you guys do for work."

"We don't need much to get by. A little PI work. I take tourists on scenic flights from time to time, too."

She gaped at him.

"In the helicopter," he hastened to clarify. "Not in dragon form. And we all do a little bodyguarding when the occasion arises."

She snorted. "Now, that, I can believe."

He wondered what she meant, but he didn't push the point lest she pry further. He, Silas, and the others did a range of work that called for their specialized skill set. Some intelligence work, some investigating. Plus, a variety of private contract work he'd rather not share the details of.

"Have you investigated me?" Tessa asked.

He nodded slowly. Carefully. "A little. Last night. Just trying to figure out why Damien Morgan targeted you."

"And what did you find?"

"Nothing. Not yet. No missing persons report filed yet, either. When is your family likely to get worried?" He'd found the records on her, her parents — divorced for decades, according to public records — and a sister on the East Coast.

She didn't answer for a long time. Too long, really.

"Not for a while," she whispered. "We're not that close."

He wanted to follow up with more questions, but her face was stony. She might as well have stuck up a *No Trespassing* sign, so he relented and changed the subject.

"So, private chef, huh? You like it?"

She nodded. "I do. Cooking for restaurants got a little boring. I like playing with recipes, seeing what clients like best."

He chuckled. "Ever think of writing a cookbook?"

He'd asked the first thing that came to his mind, but apparently, he'd struck a chord, because Tessa sighed and murmured, "Someday."

Kai wished he had the power to grab *someday* and hand it to her right there and then. She seemed so wistful, so full of hope, that his inner dragon started plotting away.

Maybe if she stayed with us a while...

"What kind of cookbook?" he asked, coaxing her along. "Do you have a specialty?"

Tessa gazed out at the sea with dreamy eyes. "Grilling. A cookbook about grilling. Something like *Gourmet Grill* or *All Fired Up*, I was thinking."

He looked at her. Whoa. She wasn't kidding.

A second later, her shoulders drooped a little. "Kind of dumb, huh?"

"Not dumb. It sounds great."

She flashed him a grin so grateful, so bright, he couldn't help smiling just as wide.

He slowed down for another turn, continued down the private road, and pulled onto the Honoapi'ilani Highway, mulling the idea over the whole time.

She can try out her recipes on the guys, his dragon said, and before he knew it, his mind filled with images of upgrading the kitchen, fetching things for her...

Whatever she needs, his dragon agreed. *We can make her happy.*

He caught himself there. His job wasn't to make Tessa happy. It was to subtly investigate her. Why did he keep drifting off task?

He checked the speed and slowed at the third turn in the road, as he always did, tossing a little salute to the left.

"Officer Meli," he murmured out of sheer habit.

"Officer who?"

He pointed left to the police car hidden at the curve.

"She's always trying to catch us speeding."

Tessa leaned forward, and he wondered how much she could see. He could picture Office Meli perfectly. Dark sunglasses. Dark hair whirled in a bun and a face that made most guys wish they could be pulled over. According to Hunter, Officer Dawn Meli's blend of Asian, Caucasian, and Polynesian features made her the most beautiful woman in the world. Kai glanced at the redhead beside him. The cop might catch Hunter's eye, but red-haired, green-eyed Tessa was more his type.

Not that he'd ever had a type, really. But the second he'd laid eyes on Tessa...

Mine, his dragon murmured.

But she was human. The closer he got to her, the more danger he put her in.

"Has she succeeded?" Tessa waved to the policewoman. "In catching anyone speeding, I mean?"

He laughed. "She gets Boone every time. I think he likes it. She catches the rest of us every once in a while. Except Hunter. He never speeds."

"Never?"

He waved a hand. "Never. Bears — you know how they can be."

She muttered something sardonic, reminding him that she'd only been thrown into the world of shifters a short time ago.

Most humans would run screaming for the hills if they learned what she had. But Tessa had an instinct for shifters, it seemed. She'd handled meeting everyone at Koa Point without batting an eye. Well, barely.

See? She can handle it. She belongs, his dragon whispered.

"And how do you know Ella?" Tessa asked.

He pinched his lips, speeding up now that the police cruiser was past. "She's a friend."

"A friend," Tessa echoed, clearly not appeased.

He shrugged. How much to say? How much to explain? Because talking about Ella meant talking about his own messed-up past.

Come on. If you can't tell Tessa, who can you tell? his dragon demanded.

No one was his preferred answer. Why tell anyone?

But Tessa looked at him with those big, green eyes, and he couldn't help but open up a bit.

"We grew up together. Not far from here." He pointed south, toward the Hana side of Maui.

"You and Ella?"

"Me, Ella, and Hunter."

"What, like a shifter commune?" Tessa joked.

He laughed, but it came out forced. "More like a home for wayward shifters. Our parents died when we were young."

Died or took off to avenge the death of a mate, as his father had done, but Kai decided to leave that part out.

Tessa's face fell. "I'm sorry. I didn't mean..."

He shrugged. "We were the lucky ones. Georgia Mae took care of us. We had all the love we could want. Not a lot of money, maybe, but she made ends meet."

"So, not on an estate like that?" Tessa jerked her thumb in the direction of Koa Point.

"I wish," he laughed.

"Is Georgia Mae a shifter, too?"

He nodded. "Was. She was an owl. She used to joke that it helped her keep an eye on us at night."

Thankfully, Tessa didn't push for more, so he didn't have to explain the details of how hard it had been to lay Georgia Mae to rest, or other things, like which of them remembered their parents — or didn't — and all the other ugly particulars of their early lives.

His dragon grew somber. *Mom. I remember Mom.*

Yeah, he remembered too. All the more reason to guard his heart now.

But that grew more difficult with every passing hour, especially with Tessa so close. Her scent wrapped around him like a silk scarf. Her voice worked its way deep into his soul, making his dragon want to hum along. The sun glinted off her hair, reminding him just how rich that color was.

Beautiful, his dragon murmured. *So beautiful.*

He fished his phone out of his pocket and handed it to her, trying to focus. First, they had to check on her luggage. Second, they had to buy food. And third, he had to collect any information on Tessa he could to try to figure out why Morgan attacked her.

Probably because she smells so good, his dragon murmured. *Because she's perfect.*

He glanced right and saw the sun glinting off her pendant. Had that attracted Morgan? It had caught his eye several times already, and Silas's, too — he'd seen his cousin peek at it then dismiss it just as he had. It was a striking stone, but obviously not the real thing. So Morgan had to have been after Tessa, not the pendant.

Tessa spoke into the phone, paused, then spoke again. "Will it be on the next flight?"

So much for her luggage, his dragon sighed.

She looked glum, but when a sign flashed by on the right, she perked up. "A farmer's market! Perfect."

He wanted to protest that the grocery store was closer and quicker, but shit. How could he take that little bit of happiness away from her?

"Farmer's market it is," he sighed, heading for the center of town.

"Wow. This is beautiful," Tessa said, swiveling her head left and right once they'd parked and started walking down the street.

Kai looked, too. Normally, he didn't take much notice of downtown Lahaina. But, yeah. The old buildings were pretty nice, he supposed. Red roofs, white trim, shaded balconies. Dozens of old-fashioned shop signs hung over the sidewalks, and pastel colors covered the walls. The town was a little touristy, but vibrant and cheery, too — much like Tessa.

"Used to be a whaler's port," he murmured, wishing he had more to tell her just to see her eyes sparkle with wonder and joy.

"Beautiful. And wow." She pulled up short, gawking at the banyan tree.

"It's some kind of historic..." he started, but she was already darting ahead, reading the plaque.

"'Planted on April 24, 1873.' Wow. Over a hundred years old."

It was a funny old tree with branches that arched up and out, then tapped back down to the ground, creating a lattice-work of trunks and roots like something out of a fantasy book.

"Like a cathedral," Tessa murmured, squinting at the sunlight filtering through the leaves.

Kai had never thought of it like that, but yeah. He could see the similarity. He glanced around, taking in the familiar surroundings with fresh eyes. It was pretty nice. A hell of a lot nicer than most places in the world, he supposed.

"This is great," Tessa said, leading him into the market sheltered under the canopy of branches and leaves.

Tables and stalls were set up like a maze, all of them exploding with color and scents. The sweet fragrance of papaya. The rough green tufts of fresh pineapple. The rich purple of cabbage. Out of nowhere, a memory jumped out at him. Georgia Mae had kept a garden, and all the kids had had to help. They'd complained at the time, but looking back, all he remembered was the smell of ripe tomatoes, the taste of fresh mango. The foresty scent of herbs and the warmth of the sun on his face.

"Can you hold this, please?" Tessa asked, breaking his reverie.

He blinked and took a deep breath. Maybe he should come to the market more often. Maybe the next time a nightmare from his active-duty days haunted him, he'd swing by here.

"Sure," he mumbled, taking the bag she thrust into his hands.

Tessa was a pro, homing right in on the pick of the crop, exchanging friendly banter with the salespeople, and complimenting them on their goods. All he had to do was follow her around like a puppy at the heels of its master. An all too apt comparison, it seemed, because his mind switched off and his senses faded until all he saw, smelled, and tasted was her.

"Excuse me." A guy backing into a stall with a wheelbarrow full of breadfruit bumped Tessa, and Kai growled. A real dragon growl he swallowed as quickly as he could.

"Did you say something?" she turned.

"Nothing. Nothing."

It was heaven, but it was torture at the same time. Having her so close — doubly close in the narrow aisles. Every time someone passed, he and Tessa had to crowd together, and their bodies kept brushing up against each other. When her shoulder touched his chest, his dragon sighed. When her hand brushed his, it was all he could do not to grasp it again. And when her rear nudged his hip, he just about groaned.

"I am going to cook you guys a dinner to remember," she murmured like she'd been reading his mind. She licked her lips, too.

Tessa's scent mixed with that of the market, and all he could think of was a different kind of feast.

She checked every aisle — twice — and once they were back in the car, she made him detour miles to the grass-fed beef butcher shop someone had tipped her off about.

"But—" he tried.

She frowned, and he threw up his hands. The woman might not be a dragon, but she sure knew how to give orders at times.

It was five before they returned to the estate where he had intended to report to Silas right away. Not that he had much to report about Tessa — other than the fact that her smile lit up his soul and her laughter was like seeing a light turn on in a tunnel and finding out it wasn't a tunnel at all, just a cage of his own making. Of course, Tessa needed help carrying the groceries first, and he tagged along just like he'd been doing all day.

"What do you call this place?" she asked when they approached the open-sided meeting house.

"Akule hale. It means meeting place."

"Akule hale," she murmured, letting the syllables flow off her tongue.

He figured he'd drop her off and let her do her thing, but damn. Tessa might have been in her element in the market, but she was an absolute queen in the kitchen, and before long, all five shifters who lived on the estate — even grim-faced Silas and that recluse of a tiger they all managed to put up with — gathered around and watched in awe.

"Wow. Someone who actually likes cooking," Boone murmured.

Kai wondered what else Tessa did with such gusto. How else he might help unleash the magic inside her soul.

"She's a pro," Hunter agreed.

Before long, Tessa had delegated jobs to each of them. Kai insisted on washing the vegetables because that put him closest to her. Hunter sharpened the knives, and Boone...

"Do I really have to cut the onions?" the wolf protested, wiping a tear from his eye.

Tessa asked Silas to set the table — which he did with a tablecloth and everything because it felt like a special occasion, even if none of them could put a finger on what that might be — and even Cruz prowled around the perimeter of the *akule hale,* sniffing as Tessa cooked.

Humans have magic, too, Georgia Mae used to say, and though Kai had never really believed her before, he did now.

The sun was setting, and its golden rays angled into the kitchen, highlighting Tessa's hair. Little tendrils curved over her forehead, and the rest swayed like a silk curtain. She tossed a salad, and when she bent her head to her shoulder to flip back her hair, he nearly reached over to stroke it. The scent of charcoal briquettes filled the air, but his nose, like the rest of his senses, focused solely on her. He leaned in closer and everything started to fade away except for Tessa's alluring scent. Closer...closer...

"Can you open this, please?" she said after a stubborn minute of struggling with a jar.

He jerked back to his senses. When he took the jar from her and popped it open, something inside him sighed at the easy domesticity of the scene. He could spend a lifetime watching Tessa and never get bored.

"So, private chef, huh?" Boone chuckled.

Yes, she is, Kai's inner dragon swelled with pride.

He'd once seen a video of a famous artist throwing paint at a canvas, turning it into a masterpiece with a couple of flicks of the wrist. Tessa was the same way. When she tossed six marinated steaks on the barbecue, every shifter groaned.

"God, that smells good," Boone murmured.

Kai took a deep whiff — of Tessa, standing just to his right, and murmured, "Sure does."

"Just a few minutes and we'll be done," Tessa said, totally unaware of the effect she had on him. Her eyes shone with joy instead of fear, and she smiled as she worked.

A drop of oil splattered, and she whisked her hand away. He nearly took her hand and rubbed it, but she showed him her unmarred skin.

"I never burn. Handy for a chef, huh?"

"Handy," he murmured, though part of him secretly wished for an excuse to stroke her skin.

Kai forced himself to step back and found the other guys grinning, too. Grinning and kicking back to watch a master at her task. Well, Silas didn't, but the rest did. Even Cruz, who disguised his smile with a lick of the lips the second he caught Kai looking.

Kai took a deep breath and glanced around. The sun was setting over the Pacific. The palms were swaying. The guys were smiling. They'd only retired from the military a few months ago, but they hadn't really relaxed until now. Cooking usually felt like a chore, as was patrolling the grounds or carrying out the odd jobs they took. But now...

We're living again. His dragon smiled.

He studied Tessa. Was it the cooking or was it Tessa that put a little gaiety back into their lives?

Then Kai caught Silas glaring at him, and he immediately wiped the dumb grin off his face. This wasn't paradise. That wasn't his mate. And whatever magic had wormed its way into their scarred corner of the world wouldn't last long.

Chapter Six

"Best steak ever," Boone said, rubbing his belly.

Tessa looked around the table. The wolf wasn't the only one who looked satisfied. All of the men did. She had to admit to feeling pretty content, too. She liked the chef business, but it had been a while since she had the chance to enjoy a meal with the people she cooked for, so the evening had been a nice change.

Like sitting next to Kai. Nice.

Well, that part was great. Having him so close made her feel peppy and alert, like something slumbering deep inside her had slowly come to life.

"Really good," Kai said, making her glow.

Going shopping with him had been fun, and he'd even eased up on his domineering ways a little. Well, okay — he had growled at a few people who'd come too close, but that was probably just the bodyguard part of him kicking into gear. And she sort of liked it — feeling special. Protected. Most importantly, he'd given in on a few points and let her have her way. So maybe he wasn't as much of a control freak as she had feared.

Not that it ought to matter, but somehow, it did. Some part of her insisted on holding out hope — for what, she wasn't sure — even though she knew they would have to part ways soon. She'd go back to living her old life — if she was lucky — and wondering whether her sojourn in Hawaii had all been a dream.

"So what's for dinner tomorrow?" Boone asked. "Or did Hunter's table manners turn you off?"

ANNA LOWE

The bear shifter raised one thick eyebrow but didn't say a word.

"Hunter's table manners?" she shot back.

Boone was the one who'd been licking his knife — unlike Hunter, who held his fork in one huge hand and the knife in the other. A bear on his best manners, as if his mother were there. The dragons, Tessa had noticed, seemed to enjoy making lamplight glint off the silverware, and she wondered if the legends about dragons with shiny hoards of treasure were true. Cruz, on the other hand, had checked the sharpness of his knife with his thumb and scowled. But somehow, he didn't intimidate her quite as much as before.

It was nice, sitting down to a meal for a change. She'd been so busy building up her business, working mornings in a breakfast café and evenings for her clients. Any spare minute was dedicated to planning ads, following up on inquiries — anything to make her business work. She'd been too busy to realize how lonely she'd been — until now.

She glanced Kai's way just as he looked at her. Had he been lonely, too?

She tore her gaze away from him before she got lost in those blue eyes all over again and dabbed her lips with a napkin. "What does everyone want tomorrow?"

Silas cleared his throat sharply, and there it was again — a reminder that she had to be on her way soon.

Tessa dropped her gaze and knotted her fingers around and around.

A heavy silence ensued until Hunter — the politest hulk of a man she'd ever met — stood and offered to clean up. When Tessa yawned behind her hand, Kai insisted on walking her back to the guesthouse.

"Sorry," she murmured. "Jet lag." Jet lag, or sheer emotional exhaustion after the craziest two days of her life.

Kai followed her out of the meeting house and into the night, walking silently at her side. Close, but not too close, which was a pity, really. Or maybe it was a good thing, considering the way her body tingled whenever they touched. Hell,

52

she tingled just from standing beside him. She just might combust into flames if they went all-out and hugged.

"You're good at what you do," Kai murmured, holding back a leafy bush for her to pass.

She slowed and brushed past him. Just one little brush, but enough to set off lightning bolts in her veins.

"I love cooking, and it's nice to have appreciative guests."

Guests sounded like the wrong word, but she could hardly call the shifters *clients*. The power-executive mother of five she cooked for was a client. The retired couple with the fancy condo on the golf course out in Scottsdale were clients. Damien Morgan had been a client, too. She wrinkled her nose. She'd been warned about checking out clients before going over to their houses, but damn. She'd been so eager for the job that she'd taken it without thinking.

"You okay?" Kai whispered. Had he been reading her thoughts again, or was the man a master of interpreting moods from body language?

She inhaled deeply, telling herself it was to savor the surrounding hibiscus and not to sneak a whiff of Kai's rich, earthy scent. Telling herself not to wish for a man — a partner, a lover — who was that in tune with her needs.

"I'm good," she whispered. "Thanks."

"Nice night," he murmured, indicating the stars.

They'd reached the shoreline, and she stood silently, not quite ready to say goodnight. Not quite able to do anything but wonder whether Kai felt the same electric zing.

He stood still as a statue, his hands shoved deep in his pockets. Tessa tipped her chin up to the stars, wishing she had the nerve to touch his hand or turn for a kiss. Just a chaste little goodnight kiss...

The sea seemed to tease her, whispering all kinds of silly ideas. And the moon — did it really have to ripple over the ocean in that peaceful, perfect-for-a-Hawaiian-honeymoon way?

She closed her eyes, counted to five, and forced herself to focus on the stars instead. The stars, the sky, and the breeze...

"I wouldn't mind being a dragon," she mused, voicing an out of the blue thought.

Kai started as if he'd never heard such a thing. But he covered up quickly. "Yeah? Why?"

She made a face then flexed her fingers in the air. "Well, I'd have the claws to put Morgan in his place, for one thing."

Kai chuckled.

Then she lifted both arms, imagining what it would be like to have wings. To fly away from bastards like Morgan. To fly to her own lair, maybe. Or just to fly, period, as she had often imagined as a kid.

"I'd love to fly on nights like these," she whispered, dipping slightly to her left as if negotiating a turn over the rippling sea. She dipped her right shoulder next, imagining what it might feel like to soar up to the moon then barrel toward the silver light dancing over the waves. A thousand tropical scents would rush up at her, giving her senses a feast. She'd steady out at the last possible second and swoop an inch away from the waves like a gull. And Kai would be right behind her, whooping and hollering with the joy of it all.

Kai cocked his head, and she dropped her arms. He probably thought she was nuts, like her sister had when she'd mentioned flying in her dreams.

He scraped the edge of the grass with his shoe. "It is nice."

She looked over. "What's nice?"

"Flying. On nights like this."

He motioned toward the water, curving his hand left and right, miming a glider. Or a gliding dragon, she realized.

She looked out over the water, fighting the emotion welling up in her chest. A wistful, achy feeling, like something had been taken from her even before she was born.

"What's it like?"

His chest lifted and fell with a deep breath, and he thought about it for a while, then spoke so quietly she had to strain to hear.

"It's nice when the sea is calm enough for the moon to reflect like that. When you fly in the beam of light, it's almost like a road. My dad used to call it the road to heaven." His voice grew soft and reverent. "He said it's the road that led him to my mom."

Tessa sighed, watching the moonshine stretch away to infinity. If only she could fly. Maybe then she could find her own soul mate.

You already found him, a little voice whispered in her mind. *Now it's time to make him yours.*

Tessa took a deep breath, telling herself not to get carried away. Balmy tropical evenings beside a hunky man with perfect manners had a way of toying with a girl's heart.

Kai cleared his throat and turned to face inland, so she did, too.

"It's fun to fly over the mountains, too. To glide over the ridgelines and follow the razor's edge."

The night was so clear she could see the sharp outline of West Maui's upper slopes, a dark line in front of an endless sky full of twinkling stars.

"That would be great," she whispered as an ankle-high wave broke across the beach, making the pebbles tumble and roll. "But don't you worry people would notice?"

Kai just shrugged. "We're careful not to show ourselves openly, but most people barely even look up, let alone pay attention to the sky. Our wings have a way of reflecting the light, so unless we fly right up to a human and breathe fire, they don't notice."

She turned, more tempted than ever to reach out and touch. To run a hand along his arm and see if she could feel the contours of a wing. To beg him to shift so she could see him in dragon form.

Or maybe she'd just touch him for the sake of a touch — a human touch. A human kiss.

His lips twitched. Was he imagining the same thing?

A moment later, she stepped back and rubbed the goose bumps on her arms.

"I guess I'd better turn in," she whispered, edging closer to the bungalow.

Kai's lips moved, and Tessa's braver half begged to hear what he had to say. The scared, almost-killed-by-a-dragon part, though, had had enough for one day.

"Thanks for everything," she murmured, stepping up to the porch.

He looked so sad, she nearly stepped back down to hug him. But then his face went expressionless again, and the moment was gone.

"Goodnight, Tessa." His voice was between a whisper and a sigh.

He stood there a moment as if willing her back then let his shoulders drop and turned to go.

"Goodnight," she whispered, slipping inside. She shut the door slowly and leaned against it, feeling hollow and tired. Her ears strained for the sound of a light rap on the door, hoping Kai might rush back to say one more thing. Or maybe even to kiss her with those amazing lips.

But there was no knock. No kiss. Just the thump of her own heart and an ache in her soul.

I'd love to fly on nights like these.

What had she been thinking, telling Kai that? She couldn't fly. She wasn't a dragon. She was suffering from shock and delusion, that's what it was.

She sighed and headed for the shower. Barbecuing had made her break into a sweat, and a shower would feel good. So she stepped into the bathroom and slipped her hands inside the waistline of the sarong, then stopped and ran her fingers over the silk. It would feel good to have Kai untie it, wouldn't it?

The X-rated part of her mind liked that idea — a lot — and followed up with even steamier ideas. Like how good it would feel to have Kai come up from behind and sniff her hair, as he'd done in the kitchen at one point.

She closed her eyes, indulging in all kinds of fantasies as she toyed with the edge of the sarong. Slowly, she slid it off. Not with one quick push the way she would do for herself, but in a long, sensual slide, the way she imagined Kai doing before he ran his hands slowly down her thighs.

She pursed her lips. A little fantasizing was okay. Why fight the pent-up sexual energy that had been building inside her all day?

After shedding the rest of her clothes — and having way too much fun with what should have been a simple act — she turned on the shower and stepped in, picturing Kai's big hand holding the soap instead of hers. She leaned against one wall of the shower, running the soap up and down, letting the water carry the suds away. Imagining was harmless, right?

She hummed and slid the soap between her breasts, following the curve of the left side up and around. Around... around...

She hummed and slid her hand in ever-tighter circles until she was bumping her own nipple.

I want Kai to do this, her body begged.

Pretend it is Kai, she told herself.

Her nipple peaked, and she circled harder then pinched, making herself gasp and writhe.

Yes. Kai, she'd say if she could.

She didn't consciously slide the soap over to the other side. It just happened, as if Kai were guiding her hand. Kai, or destiny, or some sensual Hawaiian god who liked to toy with mere mortals like her.

Leaning back against the shower wall, she let her legs inch apart, and she ran the slippery bar of soap lower. Lower. Lower...

"Yes. Kai..." she whispered, touching herself.

Her breaths grew faster and less measured until she was panting and twisting over her own hand.

"Yes... Yes..."

She probed with one finger, then two, imagining how big Kai would be. Imagining him filling her again and again. Pushing harder and harder...

She tipped her head back against the wall, jerking in more aggressive strokes. A dragon wouldn't be gentle, would he? No, he'd be a little wild, just the way she liked it.

Her head rolled as she pictured what a perfect lover Kai would be. Teasing her like this, giving her just what she needed. Giving her what no lover ever had before.

"Kai..." she panted, rocking her hips. Imagining it was Kai pinching her nipple and not her.

"Yes," she murmured, losing control. "Yes..."

Steam lifted and rolled out of the shower as her body wound tighter and tighter with need. The most urgent, most animalistic need she'd ever experienced.

"Yes," she cried, shuddering all over as the damn inside her finally broke.

A heat wave unlike any she'd ever experienced before spread through her body. She relished it. Welcomed it. Savored it, because that might be as close as she ever came to true satisfaction.

Her heart thumped a little slower, and her shoulders drooped. That wasn't Kai. That wasn't satisfaction. That was just her, imagining things.

Just her, alone.

Chapter Seven

Kai strode up the trail, dragging a hand through his hair. What was it with Tessa? What was it with him?

He pulled up and leaned against a palm like a wounded soldier who couldn't manage another step. Except he wasn't wounded. He was burning with desire.

He'd been tortured by a mild hard-on all day — one that got so bad by dinner, he'd nearly moaned. Because somewhere between Tessa squeezing the tomatoes and slathering spices over the steak, his secret fantasies went from simmering to full bonfire, and his inner dragon had worked out an entire strategy for winning over Tessa.

Take woman. Bring her to my lair. Make her mine.

The creature purred like it was the world's most perfect plan, but his human side recognized a few minor flaws.

Flaws? What flaws? his dragon demanded.

Kai sighed and closed his eyes. He'd managed to keep the beast locked in the deepest part of his conscious for most of the day, but now, the damn thing was jumping and screaming in his head. In his heart, too, not to mention in his jeans.

Must have my mate! Want to touch her. Kiss her. Make her feel good.

He closed his eyes and counted to ten.

Twenty.

Thirty.

All it really did, though, was make him grit his teeth and sweat, because that hard-on was a monster, and it was straining at his pants.

He clenched his fists and dug deeper for a miracle dose of self-control that would allow him to survive this urge. Every shifter fought with his animal side, but he couldn't let the dragon win this one.

She is ours, it hissed.

He scraped at the bark of the palm tree, gouging it with fingernails that lengthened into claws as his dragon slowly gained the upper hand.

Then Tessa's voice ghosted through his head. *His fingernails turned into claws and his ears extended. . .*

She'd turned white when she recalled Morgan's attack. Kai glared at the points of his fingernails and forced his inner dragon back.

That bastard, Morgan. . . his dragon ranted.

Do you want to be like him? he shot back.

Slowly, painfully, the burning need receded.

He stood for a few minutes then shook his head, adjusted the fit of his pants, and walked on. Stiffly at first, then a little more smoothly. Silas would already be pissed off at him for being late.

He wound up the flagstone path to his house, the second highest on the estate. Silas had the choice spot at the top of the bluff, but Kai felt more at home in his particular spot. The view stretched down the coast toward Lahaina and across the channel to Molokai. If he stood all the way on the south edge of his veranda, he could even see the thatched roof of the guest bungalow peeking out from among the trees.

The thought put a bounce in his step, but when he reached the level of his veranda, he pulled up short. Silas was there, waiting. Practically steaming from the ears, too.

"What took you so long?" Silas hissed.

Kai swung his jaw left then right, letting it click audibly as he leveled his gaze at his cousin. "I only said goodnight."

Silas's nostrils flared, and his eyes glowed. "You're far too interested in her."

"She needs protection, and I want revenge on Morgan."

"You sure that's all you want?"

No, but he'd already started stretching the truth. Might as well bend it all the way while he was at it.

"I just want to stop that bastard. What if he attacks more women? What if humans discover what he really is? He could put all of us at risk."

That argument, Silas couldn't dismiss. Plus, Kai figured, it might refocus his cousin's anger on someone else. Let Morgan be the bad guy. Hell, Morgan *was* the bad guy.

"Morgan might be a bigger problem than we thought," Silas said, turning to study the night sky.

"What do you mean?"

"I still haven't been able to contact Ella, so I started investigating Morgan's business connections and movements over the past six months."

"And?" Kai had never seen his cousin look so grim.

Silas glared at the horizon, and Kai felt a dark, ominous force creep over the tropical night.

"If they're connected at all, I suspect Morgan is more than just a low-level operator for Drax."

"Low level?" Kai snorted. "We both know how wide Morgan's reach extends and how much he controls."

Silas shook his head. "Still low level compared to Drax. Their movements parallel each other so often, I'm sure they're involved. It's all just conjecture, but the gaps in their schedules — the times no one can truly account for where they are — overlap. That, and Morgan has sent payments to a numbered account in the Caymans."

"Which could go to anyone," Kai pointed out.

"Could. I can't follow the trail any farther than that. At the same time, though, Morgan seems to have been consolidating his own power. I don't know what's worse — Morgan working for Drax, or Morgan growing bold enough to break out on his own."

Kai chewed on that for a little while. "Why Tessa, then? Why not any other human?"

Silas fixed him with a pointed look. "That's what you're supposed to be finding out."

Kai glared back. Okay, he'd spent more time enjoying her company than investigating her background. But it was important to find out who Tessa was as a person, right?

"So, get to it, already," Silas grunted, heading for the stairs. "Find out everything you can about her. I want this cleared up as soon as possible. I want her safe, but out of here. You understand that?"

Kai's dragon almost bared his teeth, but he fought his animal side back.

"What about Morgan? He could attack another woman any time."

Silas paused long enough to glare. "We'll get Morgan. One way or another, I swear we will."

I swear, too, Kai's dragon rumbled.

Silas nodded his good-bye and left with one final, *don't-get-involved-with-that-human* glare.

Kai took a deep breath to calm his dragon down and looked out over Pailolo Channel — the eight-mile stretch of water that separated Maui and Molokai. Well, he tried, but instinct kept pulling his gaze over to the roof peeking out among the trees by the beach. Was Tessa asleep? Was she worried? Was she lonely?

I'd love to fly on nights like these, she'd sighed so wistfully, it tugged on his heart.

He couldn't imagine not being able to fly. To never feel the air under his wings or soar toward the sun. He couldn't imagine being earthbound all the time.

Imagine flying with her, his dragon whispered.

He closed his eyes and leaned closer to the edge of his veranda. The drop from there was sheer, and it wasn't protected by a rail. He was a dragon, after all, and he needed a place to take off and land.

Imagine taking off with her, his dragon murmured. *We could guide her through the mountains. We could show her how we glide over the sea.*

He breathed in deeply, picturing what fun it would be. How exhilarating to share his favorite pastime with someone like her.

We could teach her how to ride the updrafts over the sea cliffs of Molokai. How to flick her wings—

Kai's eyes snapped open. Whoa. Wait. His dragon wasn't talking about taking Tessa flying. It was talking about *teaching* her to fly on her own.

She's human, he said.

We could claim her, his dragon whispered. *Make her ours. Then she could be a dragon, too.*

Are you nuts?

You know the old legends, his dragon hissed.

Of course, he knew the old legends. His father had lived long enough for him to learn dragon lore.

In the old days, plenty of dragons turned human mates, his dragon said.

That was in the old days, he pointed out. *Not in the past hundred years.*

Mating with a human was one thing, accomplished by a careful bite to the neck. But turning a human into a dragon meant puffing fire into that wound — a dangerous step his parents had never attempted.

But it could work. Wolves do it all the time. Bears, too, his dragon said.

Dragons are different. We need fire to turn our mates. Dad never risked turning Mom.

His parents had bonded for life, but his father never dared to turn his mother into a dragon. She'd been too timid to try, for one thing, and the risk was too great in his father's mind.

Maybe he should have turned her, his dragon growled. *Maybe then she would have survived.*

Kai scratched his chest then caught himself. He'd been resisting his dragon all day. Now that the sun had set, he could let his dragon out and distract it with a good, long flight. That would settle his soul enough for him to think clearly. He could work everything out of his system and research Tessa's family as soon as he returned.

Yes, his dragon hissed. *Let's fly.*

He shed his clothes quickly and dropped them on a chair, then stood at the very edge of the veranda with his toes curled over the edge. He tipped his chin up to the stars and raised his arms wide.

Fly, his dragon hummed as his body heat surged.

His blood coursed faster, and his heartbeat went from steady thumps to a quicker, staccato pace.

Fly, he agreed, spreading his fingers, giving in at last.

It hurt — the ripping sensation in his shoulders that signaled the start of a shift, but there was a thrill to it, too. A high. A burst of adrenaline. His fingers stretched painfully, but as his wings extended — wider and wider until they spanned the full width of his ledge — that, too, gave him a rush. His toes stiffened as they turned into claws. His ears pulled back as his face elongated, and his skin turned tough and leathery.

He took a deep breath and exhaled, blasting a stream of fire into the night.

I am dragon, his second side roared. *I am free.*

He let loose another ten-foot blast, then launched himself upward and off the ledge. A moment later, he was gliding over Koa Point.

Every time he flew, Kai counted himself lucky — not just to be a dragon, but to be one of the last of the mighty Llewellyn clan, like Silas. They shifted into big, powerful dragons, unlike some distant cousins who could shift but not grow past human size.

Wow. You're even bigger than an elephant, Hunter had said in awe the first time he'd witnessed Kai shift when they were both teens.

Kai had scowled at the time. Elephants were big, clunky things. Dragons were sleek. Powerful. Elegant, almost.

Fly, his dragon cried, relishing the rush of wind under his wings.

Normally, he buzzed the roof of Boone's place on his way out to sea, just for the fun of hearing the wolf complain. But tonight, he angled north to sweep over the guest cottage. Not too low, because he didn't want to startle Tessa. But not too high, so he could still sense her presence.

Just picture flying with her at our side, his dragon hummed.

He pushed the thought away — far away — and held perfectly still until he was far enough from the little cottage to beat his wings. Heading straight into the rippling line of silver water that was the moon's reflection on the sea, he smiled.

The true road to heaven, just like his father had said. But instead of following the silver line out, he found himself making a long loop until he was headed straight back the way he'd come. Straight back to Tessa.

That's the road to heaven, his dragon said. *The road to our mate.*

He wanted to protest, but the reflection did seem brighter as he skimmed the surface on this new heading. The single light in the cottage glowed, drawing him forward.

Home, a dreamy voice in his mind called. *That is home.*

It took everything he had not to pull up and land on Tessa's doorstep as his dragon demanded.

Keep flying, he insisted. *Keep flying, damn it.*

Home, his dragon chanted, barely responding. *That is home. She is home.*

Kai cursed and pounded on the thin wall between his conscience and his dragon's.

Keep flying! We can't scare her!

It was all too easy for him to imagine his dragon landing with a burst of flames, crooning to Tessa to come out. Jesus, she'd run screaming for the hills.

Need Tessa, his dragon roared. *Admit that she's our mate!*

She can't be.

Admit it. Admit it, and I'll leave the wooing to you.

Kai cursed, but what could he do?

All right! All right, already. Just keep flying.

And, *whoosh!* His dragon curled the lower edge of his wings and climbed, barely clearing the trees. In fact, his tail clipped a palm and shook the fronds furiously. But a minute later, he was shooting toward the moon and crying in glee.

She's mine! Yippee!

If Kai had been in human form, he'd have dropped his head into his hands in defeat. But he wasn't human. He was a dragon, heading for the mountains, screeching in joy.

He skimmed the lower slopes, then banked and made a loop over the Kahalawai peaks before shooting off through the lush valleys of West Maui. Just like he used to do as a kid, dodging rock formations like the Iao Needle at the last possible second just for the thrill of it.

Clearly, he'd kept his dragon leashed too long.

Maybe you've kept your heart leashed for too long, his dragon snapped back.

Obviously, the beast wasn't about to cede control. The best Kai could do was quietly, subtly, detour to the northwest.

Let's fly over Molokai, he tried. *A nice, long flight.*

His dragon's ears twitched. *We haven't been there in a while.*

We can fly along the cliffs, he said, making his voice soft. *That would be fun.*

Good idea, his dragon agreed. *We can find the best spots to take Tessa someday.*

Kai rolled his eyes, but heck. Whatever it took to wear his dragon out, he was willing to do.

Molokai, his dragon murmured, heading northwest. *Maybe even farther. We can fly to Oahu and back in one night.*

Kai made a face. Molokai was okay, but Oahu was a hundred-mile flight, and he needed time to investigate Tessa's family before dawn, when Silas would demand a report.

On the other hand, a marathon flight would tire out his dragon and shut the creature up for a while.

Sure, he said. *Oahu.*

It was a beautiful night, he had to admit. The kind of night when the sky and the sea seemed to melt together, at least from his altitude, and the islands seemed to float in midair. It was relatively calm, too, except for the crosswinds blasting off the western end of Molokai. But after that, it was all smooth flying with the lights of Oahu guiding him on. The stars twinkled overhead, and his wings felt broader than ever. His body strong, his tail long and supple. And damn, did it feel good to let his dragon push the limits once in a while.

One loop of Diamond Head, he decided as the lights of Honolulu drew near. *And then we head home.*

His dragon nodded. *Then we head home.*

He swooped over the hill, banking in line with the crater's curve, then shot back out over the sea. Molokai and Lanai were two dim lumps on the watery horizon. The trade winds had died down, making it an easy flight — until a vague sensation sounded an alarm in his mind.

He craned his long neck and spotted three dark shapes against the lights of Honolulu. He squinted, then roared.

Dragons!

He hesitated briefly. The state of Hawaii had its share of shifters, but he and Silas were the only two dragons residing in the islands. Who could those three intruders possibly be?

Dragons were highly territorial and rarely strayed far from home turf. When they did, it was mostly to wage war. Kai looked closer, wishing the moonlight would reveal more than the dull sheen of their leathery skin. One thing was clear: the dragons held their necks out, straining for maximum speed. If he maintained his easy, long-distance glide, they'd catch up in seconds. And if they'd only recently launched, they'd be far fresher.

Kai was still a good mile from land, over open ocean where he'd have space to fight. He waited a second longer then nose-dived with his wings folded tight against his sides. Just as quickly as he started the fall, he hit the brakes, spreading his wings wide to come up beneath the three strangers, catching them by surprise.

He puffed into the darkness — a single lick of fire that in dragon-speech demanded, *Friend or foe?*

He hoped for the former, but his money was on the latter, and when the three replied with long, incendiary blasts aimed at his wings, he had his answer.

Foe. Definitely foe, he decided, shooting back his own line of fire before wheeling away.

His mind spun as he roared into the night. *Who are you? What do you want?*

The snickering voice of the central dragon reached into his mind. *Who we are is of no consequence. What we want is your treasure.*

Treasure? Kai laughed, which came out as a bark in his dragon voice. Of all the dragons in the world to ambush, he and Silas were probably the least worthwhile targets. Their family had been robbed of everything. Between the two of them, Kai and Silas didn't have anything any self-respecting dragon would call a treasure. Not a proper treasure, that is.

We want your treasure, the dragon on the right added. *And we want her alive.*

Kai was so caught off guard by the remark, he hesitated a moment too long. He flinched at the sound of another eruption of flame — dragon fire that caught him on the wingtip and seared his flesh.

He roared and spun away then turned back to attack the nearest of the three. Opening his jaws wide, he steeled his wings for the kickback and called forth his own burst of flame.

Three against one, he calculated, spinning to face the second dragon. Ninety miles away from home. Shit. This was not what he'd been planning for the night.

Chapter Eight

"Whoa," Tessa murmured, sitting straight up in bed when a mighty crash sounded outside, making the ground shake.

She sat stock-still for a minute, clutching the sheets, blinking at the morning light, wondering where she was.

Her dreams had been filled with a confusing blur of images — like barbecues that turned into bonfires and raged out of control — but no loud noises. Not like the sound of a hang glider crashing through the trees and tumbling across the lawn in front of the house.

Then she remembered — this was Hawaii, not Arizona. And — oh, my — that probably wasn't a hang glider outside her door.

She threw back the sheets and ran to the front door, where she wavered for a second. What if that was Damien Morgan coming to steal her away?

But Morgan, she decided a moment later, would bellow and roar, and all she heard outside was a low, rumbly moan. Slowly, she cracked open the door and peeked.

Nothing. Not in her line of sight anyway. But the moan grew louder.

She edged a few inches out, holding on to the doorframe as if a tornado might come along and whip her away.

"Tessa." A whisper reached her ears, barely audible over the sound of the sea and the rustling foliage. The sound was so low, it would have been easy to dismiss. But instinct drew her closer, and her soul cried out. What if that was Kai? What if he was hurt? Before she knew what she was doing, she'd thrown the door wide and rushed outside.

"Kai?"

She got as far as two steps off the porch before screeching to an abrupt stop.

"Oh, my God," she whispered, backing up slowly.

It wasn't Kai. It wasn't even human, and it sure as hell wasn't a hang glider.

It was a dragon. A real-life dragon, lying crumpled on the ground.

Tessa gulped down the scream in her throat, unsure if she was more fascinated or frightened. She'd been half hoping the shifter thing was an elaborate hoax. Hoping that when Ella had shifted to fox form in front of her eyes, there'd been some kind of trick involved. But holy smokes. The creature that lay before her was as big as a truck, and its chest rose and fell with each heavy breath. Its ridged tail flicked quietly, sending pebbles tumbling over the beach, and its claws clutched at the ground.

It's in pain, she realized.

She stood frozen in place, wondering what to do. Wondering what *it* would do.

The dragon moaned. One massive wing dragged across the ground, bent at a strange angle, while the other was folded neatly across the beast's side.

Tessa. The whisper reached her mind exactly as its eyes opened, focused on her. Eyes so blue, they rivaled the sky.

She stiffened, and her breath caught.

"Kai?"

He blinked, and her heart jumped into her throat. It really was him. And whoa — he really was a dragon shifter.

Her heart thumped the way it had when she'd first met him at the estate gate — hard and heavy, along with an achy sensation under her ribs and a yearning she couldn't explain.

One second, she was rooted to the ground. The next, she rushed up to him and fell to her knees. "Kai..."

His muzzle was almost as big as her torso, but her fear had vanished, replaced by the instinct to hold and help. How badly was he hurt? Was he dying?

"Keep still," she murmured, touching one of his long, tapered ears. Marveling at how silky it felt despite the weather-hardened appearance. Crying at the pain she could sense.

She scanned his huge body, trying to make out the nature of his injuries, but her mind kept stalling out on the basics.

Wings. Kai has wings.

Great, sectioned wings that looked remarkably delicate despite their sheer expanse. A broad, armored chest that rose and fell with every heated exhale, and a ridged neck. All that and incredibly blue eyes that gazed at her in a mixture of wonder and relief.

"Kai," she whispered, rubbing his ear.

She couldn't make out any details, only that patches of his leathery skin were darker than others. Was that blood? And the wing — was it broken?

A low, rumbly sound echoed through the ground, and she jerked away. But the sound stopped, too, and that wave of yearning swept over her again as if leaving an inch between her body and Kai's was too much. As if she belonged there with him.

When she reached out gingerly and started stroking his ears again, the rumble resumed and Kai sighed.

That rumble wasn't a growl of warning. It was a dragon's version of a purr. He liked being petted.

And damn, she liked it, too. Her body warmed, and if it hadn't been for his injuries, she'd have been tempted to curl up beside him.

She kneeled, touching his ears, trying to process the jumble of emotions inside. Fear. Wonder. Worry. Love.

Whoa. Wait a minute. Love? She stared at her hand as it moved over his ears.

She was probably just mixed up. Still in shock over all that had transpired in the last twenty-four hours. That had to be it, right?

But the ache inside her grew and grew, and she found herself moving closer to the dragon.

Closer to Kai, her soul whispered deep inside.

She closed her eyes, still stroking his ears, telling herself she wasn't crazy. Just a little mixed up. Running for help seemed like a sensible option, but she couldn't drag herself away. She couldn't think clearly at all, as if she was in a bubble, apart from the world. Apart from everything but Kai.

He pressed into her hand, begging for her to continue. A minute ticked by, and the warmth between them grew steadily, filling her with comfort and hope. Time ticked to a stop, and every breath stretched to infinity. Tessa kept her eyes shut tightly, because she'd never felt anything so magical in her life.

But then Kai groaned again, and her eyes snapped open.

"Oh," she breathed as reality set back in.

He was human again. Human and sprawled on his side, with his bare back covered in gashes and blood.

"Kai," she cried, touching his shoulders, wondering if she'd just imagined the dragon part.

"Tess. . ." he murmured.

"Oh, my God. Kai." The words stuck in her throat and recycled themselves a half-dozen times as she tried to calm herself down.

His hair was matted and mussed, and a long, dark burn line extended down his back. Down, down, and down, right to—

"Oh, my," she said, half whisper, half gasp.

He wasn't just bare-chested. He was bare everything. And any inch of his tanned, toned body that wasn't smudged with blood or soot was scratched, or worse.

She nearly asked, *What happened?* but decided she'd rather not know. Not when she had more important things to do. She dashed back to the porch to grab a towel, then returned to Kai's side, ready to stem the flow of blood in the worst of his wounds.

"Get Silas," Kai said in a voice as dry and cracked as his lips.

"I need to stop the bleeding first."

"I'm okay," he croaked.

"You sure don't look it. Now hold still."

72

She checked the biggest gash, but the blood was mostly dried. In fact, the wound was already closed. The scratches all around it were healing, as was the tear across his lower back.

"I'm fine," he rasped, rolling to his side.

He certainly wasn't fine, although he wasn't the oozing mess she'd feared. She threw the towel over his hips — not that he seemed the least bit embarrassed by his nudity. More like she was.

Her necklace swung out from her neck when she knelt, catching the morning light. Kai reached up and touched the pendant.

"Same color as your eyes," he whispered. "Beautiful."

His eyes were glowing again — deep blue fringed with mesmerizing little yellow sparks — and his hand cupped her cheek. Tessa covered his hand with hers and held her breath. A whale could breach right out of the ocean behind them, and she wouldn't be able to tear her gaze away from Kai. The outside world grew muted and far away, and all she could hear was the rush of blood in her veins.

"Tessa," he whispered. But then his eyes slid shut, and his head tilted to the ground.

"Kai!" She squeezed his hand, then shook his shoulder. "Kai!"

Panic welled up in her, but she gulped it down. She'd be no help if she turned into a blubbering mess. What she had to do was remember whatever it was she'd learned in that first aid course, so long ago. Something about checking the scene and checking breathing, right?

She kneeled down and saw a blade of grass stir under Kai's breath. He'd passed out, but he was alive. What next?

Calling for help. She had to find someone. She looked around. Which of the other men lived closest? Where were they? Reluctantly, she pulled away from Kai and sprinted up the path. And damn, she'd never been so happy to see Silas, musing over a mug of coffee in the open-sided meeting house as just then.

"Help! Kai is hurt. Please help."

Within minutes, Silas and Boone were kneeling at Kai's side.

"Kai," Silas growled, shaking him roughly.

"Hey! He's hurt."

"Not that hurt."

Tessa gaped. A second later, her vision went red, and a switch in her flipped. Before she even knew what she was doing, she'd grabbed Silas's shoulder and shoved him back. He sat, ass in the grass, blinking up at her.

Everything went very, very quiet, and Boone muttered, "Oh, shit."

Somehow, his comment fueled her anger again, and Tessa thrust her hands to her hips.

"He's hurt. Are you going to help him, or should I do it myself?"

Boone stepped back. Silas glowered.

"We heal quickly," the dragon shifter said as his tanned face turned a deep shade of red.

"Do you? I wouldn't know," she said, refusing to back down. "All I know is that there's a hell of a lot of blood on his body and a couple of very serious gashes."

Silas jumped to his feet in one quick, effortless motion and stepped right into her space, staring her down. "There are many things you don't know about the world of shifters, Miss Byrne."

"I know that's no way to treat an injured man," she shot back, refusing to be cowed. Later, she'd let her knees knock and her teeth chatter at the power and anger she sensed sloughing off Silas. But not now.

They stood staring each other down until Hunter lumbered down the path, creating enough of a ruckus with his size that the impasse was broken.

"Carry him," Silas muttered, stepping away from Tessa.

Hunter took Kai's shoulders, and Boone grabbed his feet while Tessa fussed from alongside. She did her best to keep the towel looped over Kai, too, which made Boone grin.

"Don't worry, sweetheart. Shifters ain't modest."

Shifters might not be, but she sure as hell felt funny gawking at a naked man — even if the man in question was the one she'd been fantasizing about hours earlier.

"And the next time you're injured, Boone?" she asked, arching an eyebrow at him.

He laughed. "Then I hope you're here to take care of me, sweetheart."

She nearly smiled, but then frowned, because the likelihood of there being a next time was slim. She'd be on her way soon, for one thing, and she really didn't want to see any of these men hurt, for another. Not even Silas, as much as he rubbed her the wrong way.

Kai was a big man, but Hunter and Boone carried him easily. They followed a winding path up the steep slope of the estate. A stream skipped along the flagstone path, the edges overgrown with flowers and leafy bushes she couldn't name. When they reached what had to be Kai's house, Tessa stopped and gawked for a moment. The view was spectacular, and so was the house. Stone walls squared off by huge expanses of glass backed into the cliff, retreating into a dwelling that was part Frank Lloyd Wright, part dragon's lair. Rather than windows, the entire front was made of sliding glass doors, and they were all pushed open, welcoming in the sky and the light.

"Watch out," Boone muttered as they maneuvered Kai onto the couch.

Tessa followed them inside. The place was imposing from the outside, but it was cozy inside, with colorful rugs and framed images on the walls — one of a lush, mist-covered mountain, another of a yellow flower, growing beside a rock.

Silas stood frowning at the door for a while, then motioned the others out.

"You." He pointed at Tessa. "Stay if you insist. But you'll see that he's all right."

He spun and walked away.

Boone waggled his eyebrows before following Silas. "Go at it, Nurse Tessa. You've got your patient all to yourself."

She caught her protest a minute before it left her lips. She'd insisted on helping, so here she was.

She ran a hand over Kai's forehead. His breathing was steady, and his wounds were no worse than before. In fact, the longest gash was already scabbing over. But he was still a mess, and she wasn't going to let him lie there in that state.

She set off, roaming the house for supplies. The living room was airy and sparsely furnished. The kitchen was a gleaming, modern expanse with white counters and white doors. The bedroom—

She gulped and forced her eyes away from the king-size bed with its tangled sheets. Too late, though — her dirty mind was already spinning with a dozen intimate images.

"Bathroom," she murmured, ordering her legs onward.

The bathroom was huge, with a spacious, blue-tiled shower she would have loved to try out. Like the rest of Kai's home, it was a little bare but orderly, with shaving utensils lying enough out of place to give the space a homey feel rather than something from a photo shoot.

She grabbed a towel from the bathroom and a bowl of warm, soapy water from the kitchen and proceeded to wipe Kai's skin clean.

Silas was right. Kai seemed fine. Slumbering, not suffering, as she'd initially feared.

She rose and stepped back, watching him for a minute. He looked ten years younger now that he was at rest. All the worry he carried with him, all that... that — whatever it was he kept bottled up inside — was gone, at least temporarily. She reached out, brushing a finger along the sharp line of his eyebrow, tracing the upward curve.

Okay, Tessa, she caught herself. *Quit drooling. Quit dreaming. Get on with it.*

She forced herself to step back and look around the strange mix of bare-bones bachelor pad and fancy lifestyle magazine. The furniture was all hardwood with smooth, creamy tones. The floor-to-ceiling bookshelf was filled with beautiful books, and every window was hung with a glass ornament of some kind that caught and reflected the light. She walked over to one and touched it gingerly. The glass bauble seemed impossibly fragile, the blue color practically alive. The next window had a yellow ball like a tiny, tropical sun, and the next—

She stopped and held her breath. In the next window hung an emerald pendant exactly the color of her necklace.

Same color as your eyes, Kai had said. *Beautiful.*

She held her pendant up to the one hanging in the window and turned it this way and that, doubling the green splotch it cast against the white wall of the room. They were different shapes and sizes, but the color was exactly the same.

"Beautiful," she whispered.

The beam of green light lit a framed photo of a young boy with a happy couple. The woman had Kai's blue eyes, and the man had his upswept eyebrows. Kai with his parents. Tessa touched the frame gently then pulled away. There was something intensely private about the photo — private and sad. She turned away with a sigh.

The rest of the house — what there was of it, because it looked bigger from the outside than it really was — was also decorated with colorful baubles, and she couldn't help wondering whether that was a reflection of Kai's personal taste or whether all dragons liked shiny, beautiful things that infused their world with energy and light.

A spiral staircase wound upward, and she padded the stairs quietly, wondering where they led. Another room? A rooftop deck?

The latter, as it turned out, and she whistled at the view. The neighboring islands seemed bigger and closer from up there, and she swore she could make out a glimpse of Oahu between Molokai and Lanai. She stood at the edge, closed her eyes, and spread her arms wide. What would it be like to be able to fly? To turn and soar and glide over the mountains and the sea?

The breeze teased her hair as childhood dreams rushed out of the dark recesses of her memory and into the present, telling her how easy flying would be. All she had to do was curl her fingers slightly to bank left or right. To climb upward, all she'd have to do was tilt her chin up and head for the sky.

ANNA LOWE

It felt so real. So vivid. So achievable. But then she opened her eyes and remembered. Those weren't wings flapping — it was just the movement of her sarong in the wind. And the cool kiss of upper altitude air on her cheek was just the pinch of the sea breeze.

She sighed and backed away from the edge, suddenly sheepish. She'd better get down before anyone noticed her acting like a shifter wannabe.

Kai was breathing easily, and his wounds weren't a fraction as bad as they'd been before. Tessa wanted to pull up a chair and watch. Could a dragon shifter heal before her very eyes? But she felt too much like a voyeur watching him sleep, so she stepped out to the main veranda and looked out again, standing at the edge to feel closer to the sky. Would she ever understand shifters? Did she want to?

A scuffing sound dragged her gaze around to the right, where Boone was coming up the stairs.

"Hi," the wolf murmured, eyeing her strangely.

"Hi," she whispered so as not to disturb Kai. But Boone hardly seemed to glance Kai's way at all. He just stared at her.

"What?" she demanded a second later.

Boone shook his head quickly. "Not afraid of heights, huh?"

He pointed at her feet. Oh. There was kind of — well, a cliff there and no rail. She'd barely noticed, somehow.

"No, not afraid of heights," she murmured, backing up slowly. She glanced at the upper level and realized there was no guardrail there either.

Boone's eyes drifted to her neck, and she reached up to touch her pendant while he murmured a vague *Hmm* sound.

"What?" she asked. It was just a cheap pendant her grandmother had given her.

He snapped his eyes away. "Nothing. How's our patient?"

She nodded. "Better. I think." But then she pictured the extent of Kai's wounds when she'd first found him and winced. "Has he really been hurt worse?"

Boone shrugged. "Yep. We all have."

She frowned, wondering why, where, when. Wondering if she really wanted to know.

"Bet it still hurts, though."

Boone's brow furrowed, and he rubbed his abdomen absently — the spot of an old wound? "I'll save you the gory details, shall I?"

She gulped and nodded.

"Let's just say it hurts like hell. But we heal." His voice was cavalier, but his eyes gave the truth away. "Anyway," he went on quickly. "The airline called. They found your bag. Want me to take you to pick it up?"

She paced back over to check on Kai and stood there deciding for a moment, reaching up to touch one of three colored baubles as she did.

Boone snorted behind her. "Dragons. They sure do like their shiny things."

She looked up at the row of three suncatchers. One red, one orange, one yellow. The color of fire.

I like shiny things, too. She smiled, turning to look at another set of two hanging farther away.

Boone chuckled. "Shiny things, precious things. And no sooner do they have one than they want another."

She looked at Kai again, not keen to leave him alone. But he did seem all right, and the thought of having her things again — the few possessions she'd grabbed in her rush to flee Phoenix, that is — made her nod quickly and follow Boone down to the driveway and along the row of cars.

He hung a left at one arch of the garage, grabbed a helmet, and pointed to a motorcycle. "Ready to ride?"

The sleek black-and-chrome bike looked like it could zip her to the other side of the island in five minutes flat. But she hung back, in part at the idea of riding that close to anyone but Kai — no, thanks — as well as at the practical aspect.

"Not exactly space for a suitcase, is there?"

Boone sighed and put down the helmet. "Fine. We'll take the Lamborghini."

She snorted. "Sure. Why not the Lamborghini?"

ANNA LOWE

She didn't so much step into the low-riding vehicle as crouch and slide, then sat there, afraid to touch any part of the leather interior.

"Nice," she murmured. "Is it yours?"

Boone laughed out loud as he hit the gas and sped backward out of the garage. The tires squealed, and the turn pushed Tessa against the door.

"I wish," Boone said, throwing it into forward. "But I get to use it."

"Nice," she murmured, wondering about the arrangement at this estate. Was the owner a rich shifter who worked around the world like Damien Morgan?

In minutes, Boone had peeled out of the driveway and onto the main road. The car was so fast, she didn't realize how fast they were going until she noted the coastline whip past.

"Um, aren't you going a little—"

"Damn," Boone muttered as red and blue lights flashed from behind. "Officer Meli."

Tessa looked back, trying to place the name. "Who?"

He sighed. "Officer Meli. She always gets her man. Even if he's the wrong man."

Tessa wondered what that meant but remained quiet as a mouse as Boone pulled over and rolled the window down.

"Aloha," he called cheerily.

When the policewoman bent at the window, her thick braid rolled over her shoulder. It was the same Asian-island beauty Tessa remembered seeing before.

"Mr. Hawthorne," the officer said without reading his license.

"Officer Meli. How fast today?

"Seventy in a forty zone."

"New record?"

"Hardly."

Boone grinned. "I'll try harder next time."

Officer Meli ripped the ticket out of her notepad and handed it over. "Please don't."

Boone waved good-bye and drove away at half his previous pace. The second they were around the first turn, he sighed

80

and tossed the ticket into the back seat where Tessa spotted several more.

"Don't those get expensive?"

He shrugged. "Probably."

She cocked her head. "Are you that rich?"

He snorted. "Me? No."

"Is Silas? Or the estate owner? How does that work anyway?"

Boone pursed his lips and eased the car into third gear, hitting the speed limit in five seconds flat. "Look. I like you. I'd love to tell you what you want to know. But I can't, even if I, personally, trust you."

"Meaning the others don't?" She thought of Silas with his stern face and Cruz with his wary tiger's gaze.

"Let's just say they have their issues with humans."

"And you don't?"

He laughed. "Oh, I have issues. Just not with humans."

She scrutinized him. "So is Silas the owner of the estate?"

He flapped a hand over the steering wheel. "I wish I knew."

"You don't know?"

He shook his head. "Look, we all have our secrets. Him. You. Me—"

She raised a hand in protest. "I don't have secrets."

His gaze dropped to her neck. "You sure about that?"

She furrowed her brow and touched her pendant. What was he talking about?

Before she could ask, he went on. "Listen, you want to know about Silas's finances, you can ask him. You'd better brace yourself, though, because his people skills are a little lacking. Of course, he is a dragon." Boone grinned. "Me, last I checked, I had $586 in the bank. But that was a few months ago, so who knows."

Tessa folded her hands in her lap and looked over the Pacific, glittering under the sun on her right.

"Tell me about dragons," she said.

He looked at her, letting the car's speed inch up again. "What do you want to know?"

"Like why Morgan would want a mate."

Boone sputtered in surprise. "Morgan said that?"

Tessa nodded, watching the wolf closely.

He kept his eyes on the road and grew serious for the first time. "Dragons are like most shifters. They believe in destined mates."

"Destined mates?" Her pulse quickened as the words zipped around her mind. Why did they sound so familiar?

Boone's hands opened and closed around the wheel. "Like a soul mate, I guess." He was trying to sound casual, she could tell, but not really succeeding. "But more, too. Someone you love and protect and cherish forever. The one person in the whole world who really understands you. Someone who—" The words bubbled out of him until he shut his mouth abruptly. "Something like that, anyway."

Tessa stared. Did Boone have a mate? Had he lost her?

"Forever?" she whispered, thinking of Kai.

Boone gnawed his lip before answering. "A lot of shifters believe that nonsense. That there's only one person out there for you, and when you find her. . . "

He let the silence hang for a moment, then cleared his throat.

"First time in Hawaii?" he asked, changing the subject abruptly.

Tessa studied his profile then gave in.

"First trip to Hawaii." Would it be her last, too?

She spent the rest of the drive in silence, as did Boone. Tessa's mind bounced from Kai to Morgan and back again all the way to the airport. Seeing her suitcase gave her a ridiculously giddy rush, and she was tempted to clutch it in her lap the whole way back to Koa Point. That bag was hers. The things in it were hers. The second Boone dropped her off at the guest cottage, she ran inside, opened the suitcase, and started touching her things, reassuring herself, just as Boone had reassured her that it would be better to leave Kai alone for a while longer. She sat on the floor and picked up her favorite blue shirt just because she could. Because she had that little bit of control back. Her best sandals were in there, too, along with her diary and her prize possession — her grandmother's leather-covered cookbook. She hugged it tightly, then kissed the worn cover and set it aside.

Clean underwear — three whole pairs — were a huge bonus, as was her favorite pair of jeans. When she lifted them out, the brown cardboard corner of a box poked up from the bottom of the suitcase, and she lifted it out. She'd grabbed the mail on her flight from her apartment. Ella had hurried her the whole time, and that little package had been among the bills and letters she'd received.

She sat on the bed and studied the return address.

"Aunt Frieda?"

She'd never been close to that side of the family. In fact, she'd found it hard to feel close to either side of the family after her parents' bitter, drawn-out divorce when she was a kid. Still, it was nice to hear from someone every once in a while.

It took some work, but she ripped the tape apart and opened the box, where there was a note and a small wooden box inlaid with mother-of-pearl that shone in the sun.

Hello Tessa,

I've been going through a few last things of your grandmother's. She wanted you to have this. Hope you're doing well and that the cooking business is good.

Love, Frieda.

Tessa held the box, wondering what her aunt might say if she wrote an honest reply.

Cooking business was going well until I was attacked by a dragon. Currently in Hawaii. Not sure what I'll do next...

She sighed and opened the clasp of the box. Funny how the plain rosewood felt a little warm to the touch. Maybe that side of her suitcase had been facing the sun on the drive back from the airport. She held the box up to her nose, sniffed the wood, and smiled, because it smelled like her grandmother's house. Her refuge — her home away from a confused home throughout high school and college. She'd visited regularly in the six years since, right up until her grandmother's death six months ago.

Her grandmother had gifted her the cookbook in person, three years earlier, but never mentioned this box. Tessa remembered it vaguely — one of many cluttering the top of her grandmother's shelves back home. What might be inside?

She popped the top open, spread the silk handkerchief padding the inside, and stared.

Chapter Nine

Kai groaned and turned slowly from his side to his back. He'd been drifting around in the world's most beautiful dream — a dream of him and Tessa, lying on a sandy beach. Palms swayed overhead, splitting the sun's rays into a dozen separate streams of light that played over their naked bodies and made Tessa's pendant glow. She was kissing his chest, and when she looked up at him, her eyes glowed just like a dragon's. She *was* a dragon in that dream, and there was no reason why he couldn't love her.

And the best part of the dream? Time stood still, and they were totally unrushed. Gone was the niggling sense of fate about to dive in and tear his world apart. Gone was the ticking of a clock, counting down to some precipitous event. It was just him and her with nothing between them. Nothing to hold back the burning, desperate need.

Mate, a deep, earthy voice whispered in his mind. *She is your mate.*

Mate, Tessa echoed. *Make me your mate.*

But from one second to the next, the dream vanished, and he was awake. Awake and aching from every damn sinew of his body. He blinked and looked around. No Tessa, though he could have sworn she'd been there. No beach. No emerald shining as bright as her eyes. Nothing but the sunlight streaming through the windows of his house.

How he'd even gotten there, he had no clue. The last thing he remembered was squinting through burning pain to find his way home and somehow land without taking out an acre of trees.

He bent his right arm gingerly and grimaced. That was the side that had sustained the worst damage in the fight. His elbow hurt, but he could bend it. His wrist worked, too — more or less. So, really, he'd gotten off okay.

Slowly, he sat up. What time was it? And more importantly, where had those three dragons come from?

We want your treasure. And we want her alive.

Her. Tessa?

He leaned over his knees and took a couple of deep breaths before standing up. None of the dragons who'd attacked him had been his equal, but they'd used their three-to-one advantage well.

Up until the green one made a crucial mistake, his dragon grinned.

That memory, he liked. The green-hued dragon was the smallest and fastest of the three, cutting and wheeling so quickly, Kai could barely keep track of the bastard. The other two blasted away with long bursts of flame, while the smaller one darted between them. But they kept attacking in the same pattern, and as soon as Kai figured it out, greenie was toast.

Literally.

Kai had waited until the last possible second to fold his wings and dive to one side, which put greenie straight in the line of fire of the big red one. The dragon had careened into the sea with a splash while Kai shot straight back up and caught the red one from behind with a huge burst of flame.

My treasure! he'd roared when the single survivor beat a hasty retreat. *Mine!*

Tessa was his and his alone. It had been so startlingly clear in the thick of the fight and over the long flight home through the dark. But, shit. Everything was harder to make sense of in the harsh light of day. Tessa was human.

Just like Mom, he reminded his dragon. *The closer she stays to us, the more danger she's in.*

Those dragons were hunting her. Demanding her. She's already in danger, his dragon pointed out.

He scratched his head. Usually, his human side was the logical part. Why was his dragon the one suddenly making sense?

Because you worry too much. You think too much about the past.

Kai pushed to his feet, closing his eyes against the pain.

"What happened?"

Kai looked up to find Silas staring at him from the doorway with an expression as harsh as the tone of his voice. Ah, his dear cousin. So forgiving. So willing to give a guy a break.

Not.

Kai sank back down to sit on the edge of the couch and rolled his head left then right.

"Where's Tessa? Is she all right?"

Silas nodded, sour as ever. "Her luggage arrived. Boone took her to pick it up."

"Boone?" Kai jumped to his feet, ignoring the pain knifing through him as he dashed toward the door.

Silas caught his arm, sending fireworks through the right side of his body. "She'll be fine."

"Fine? Fine?" Kai sputtered for a while, unable to put his rage into words. He could kill Boone. "That damn wolf has no right going anywhere with my mate."

"Mate?" Silas retorted, going perfectly still.

Kai went still, too. Had he just said that?

Sure did, his dragon hummed. *The moonlight led us to her. Don't you remember?*

He remembered his mind going so hazy that he'd nearly flown into the cliffs of Molokai. And he remembered being so disoriented that he'd nearly let the wind blow him to Lanai instead of Maui. But then the sea had glimmered, and a voice just like his father's whispered in his head.

The road to heaven. The path to your mate.

And there it was — a silvery highway, leading him home. If he'd had an extra ounce of energy, he would have glanced around for the ghost of his father or the shadow of destiny. But all he could manage at that point was to keep beating his wings until the peaked roof of Tessa's cottage came into view.

Mate. She is our mate.

He shook Silas off and rushed to grab some clothes. "Damn it, how could you let her leave the estate? She's in danger."

"You're the one who came home covered in blood. What happened?"

"I need to see her."

"She'll be fine with Boone," Silas insisted.

"Fine if a couple of dragons swoop out of nowhere to attack her?" Kai stepped out onto the veranda and scanned the sky.

Silas's voice dropped an octave. "What dragons? Where?"

Maui was their territory, as was all of Hawaii by extension, because dragons ranged far and wide. Hell, Silas had flipped out two years ago when an aging old dragon petitioned to spend six months a year on the Big Island. If that dragon hadn't been a distant relative, Silas never would have allowed it.

Of course, Damien Morgan was a distant relative, too. Kai scowled.

"Three of them. They took off from Oahu to attack me in Ka'iwi Channel. Smart enough to keep the fight out of human sight."

Dumb enough to think they could take me, his dragon huffed.

"Who?"

Kai shrugged — and immediately regretted it. His left side was doing okay. His right side, not so much.

"No one with local knowledge, that's for sure. They didn't take the back eddies off the windward side of Oahu into account."

Silas nodded slowly. "Shifters from the mainland, then."

Kai considered. "Could be. They're after Tessa. They said, 'We want your treasure. And we want her alive.' *Her,* Silas. They said *her.*"

"Who would consider that human a treasure?"

Kai whirled and took three thunderous steps, coming face-to-face with Silas. He almost grabbed his cousin by the front of the shirt and shook him, too.

"Watch what you say."

Silas didn't push him back; he just stared into Kai's eyes. "You really think she's your mate?"

Kai stepped away, looked over the sea, and whispered, "Yes."

His soul cried because he should be celebrating and shouting that to the sky. If only it weren't all so complicated — and so dangerous for Tessa to get involved with him.

Silas's dark eyes bored into his, unrelenting. But Kai stared right back. Tessa was his mate. Silas needed to accept that. The others would have to, as well. And then... Shit. Somehow, he'd have to explain to Tessa, too.

She feels it, too, his dragon whispered. *She wants us the way we want her.*

That much was simple — deceptively simple. He doubted Tessa wanted anything to do with the shifter world — especially considering his mother's fate.

"She might not have a choice," Silas growled.

Kai looked up quickly, chagrined that he'd let his thoughts slip far enough for Silas to read them. Chagrined and alarmed.

"What do you mean?"

"Obviously, there's more to her than meets the eye. Why would three dragons be after her, calling her a treasure?"

It sounded like a rhetorical question, but Kai couldn't puzzle it out. All he could do was gnash his teeth at the thought of that rich bastard, Morgan. "You think Morgan has the resources to send three dragons out after her?"

Silas tilted his head this way and that. "Morgan may or may not have battalions of dragons at his command." His eyes flashed. "But Drax sure does."

Kai growled at the thought of their archenemy, and the sound vibrated through his chest. "What would Drax have to do with this?"

"Could be that necklace she wears," Silas said. "The one that looks just like the Lifestone."

Kai thought the pendant looked familiar, but he hadn't been able to put his finger on it until now.

The Lifestone, Kai's dragon breathed. One of a group of legendary gems long lost to dragonkind.

He shook his head before his dragon got carried away with the idea. "It only looks like the Lifestone. Look closer, and it's easy to spot as a fake."

"Still, that could be what attracted Morgan's attention. And on the off-chance that Drax is involved..."

"Why would he be interested in a copy of the Lifestone?"

"He wouldn't be. He'd want the real thing. But maybe the copy is a clue. Maybe it can lead us to the real thing. Did you find out where Tessa got it?"

Kai shrugged. "Her grandmother gave it to her." He hadn't just been dreaming about Tessa the previous day, after all. He'd managed to collect a few facts, too.

"Her grandmother?"

Kai frowned. He'd been meaning to research that side of Tessa's family, but he'd ended up flying all night, trying to cool off his dragon. And damn, he'd accomplished the opposite. His inner beast was hungrier for Tessa than ever. Surer than ever that they could somehow make it work.

"Don't tell me you didn't research it yet," Silas snarled.

Kai scuffed the floor with his shoe. No, he hadn't. Yet.

Silas shook his head, then gripped Kai's shoulder and spoke quietly. "There's another possibility as to why Morgan wants her, and that troubles me even more. She could be a fire maiden."

Kai went perfectly still. *Fire maiden* — a human who could bear a dragon shifter's child. Could Tessa be one of the very few, like his mother had been? He'd love Tessa either way, but to others, the difference was huge.

"Fire maiden," he whispered, wondering if it could be true. Fire maidens were so rare, they were coveted and revered — if not always for the right reasons.

"Drax would give anything for a woman who could bear him a shifter child. Morgan, too," Silas said.

His dragon wanted to correct Silas. *It would be Tessa's child. Hers and mine, if we're that lucky one day.*

Kai shook his head. Stupid dragon, getting ahead of himself again.

But now that the thought had arisen, it danced around his head. Him. Tessa. Together, making a family. Dragon numbers were dwindling all over the world. They had been for centuries. Some male dragons were lucky enough to find a woman they loved — shifter or human. Others spent a lifetime wishing — or warring for one of the few who could carry on their dragon line.

His mouth grew hot, the taste sulfurous. No one would take his mate from him. No one.

Silas went on, making Kai's blood boil. "Drax is on a mission to dominate all dragons, but even he is mortal. And he has no heirs — no shifter heirs, anyway."

Kai rolled his eyes. He didn't want to imagine how many women a man like Drax had bedded — but the few humans who became pregnant from a dragon partner bore human offspring — worthless to a man like Drax.

Wouldn't be worthless to me, Kai's dragon cried. *I'd love any child. I'd protect it to the death.*

Sadly, most dragons didn't see it that way and ignored their human offspring. The ruthless, power hungry dragons. The ones with the resources to hunt down and capture whatever they coveted. Like Tessa.

Whether it was Morgan or Drax who was after Tessa, he didn't care. He'd protect her with his life. He'd do whatever it took.

"I have to talk to her," he said, turning for the stairs.

But, shit. What would he say? And how would he explain himself? He'd spent most of the morning recovering from his injuries, not protecting his mate, who'd left the estate with Boone. Boone!

His dragon growled, and the anger came back. Forgetting his pain, he stormed out, growing angrier with every step. Angry with Boone. With Silas. With Damien Morgan. And most of all, with himself. He ought to have been guarding Tessa last night, not indulging in a flight.

Good thing we did, his dragon snorted. *We kept the battle away from Tessa. Better to fight far away than in front of her eyes.*

He checked the sky for fleet, gliding shadows and hurried on.

"Damn it—" Silas cursed.

Kai hurried onward, ignoring him, and Silas didn't follow. He did shoot one thought into Kai's mind, though.

Think about it, hotshot. What are you going to tell her?

Kai gnashed his teeth as he hurried toward the guesthouse. He had no clue. But he'd think of something, right?

Chapter Ten

Tessa tilted her grandmother's box, gaping as sunlight bounced off the gem within. It was so beautiful — so impossibly brilliant — she was afraid to touch it. Instead, she fingered the pendant around her neck.

She was just working up the nerve to touch the stone in the box when footsteps stormed over the porch — so loud and insistent that she dropped the box in surprise. It landed in the soft cushion of clothes in her luggage as she spun toward the door.

"Kai," she whispered as a jolt of electricity went through her.

He's all right! He's all right! He's come to see me! Her soul rejoiced.

She hurried over, touching his arm. "Are you okay?"

Her body lit up with a thousand watts of joyous energy at the sight of him. But, whoa. His eyes were blazing — red, not blue — and his fists were clenched at his sides.

"What's wrong?"

"Are you okay?" he demanded. *Demanded* without a hint of tenderness.

She took a step back. Why was he angry? What had she done?

"Of course I'm okay. You're the one who was hurt."

"You're the one who took off with that goddamned wolf," he thundered.

Holy cow — Kai was jealous?

"The airline called. Boone took me to pick up my suitcase—"

Kai closed the distance between them. "You know how dangerous it is out there for you?"

He stood at full height, and man, did his shoulders seem a mile wide. The power pulsing off him ought to have scared her to death, but her confusion became consternation. The warm, happy feeling in her gut turned into a raging anger that threatened to sweep her away.

Count to ten, her grandmother's words echoed through her mind.

She didn't want to count to ten. She wanted — needed — to get mad. Mad in a way she rarely did, but when the urge took over, it was like a hidden second soul rearing up inside.

"I decide where I go and when. And you, incidentally, were hurt. Sleeping, as a matter of fact."

"I wasn't—" he started, but she cut him off.

"I woke up to you crash-landing on my front lawn. I took care of you." The rage spun higher and higher, like a tornado just beginning to form, and she shoved him back — hard. So hard, he blinked. "I worried my ass off that you were okay."

That seemed to get his attention, so she shoved him again, a step back for every statement she made. "What gives you the right to tell me what to do?"

A red haze fell over her vision as a slew of dark memories came back. Of her mother, deciding which friends she could and couldn't see. Of her older sister, insisting her dreams were nonsense. Of her father, snorting that she'd never make it as a chef. Telling her she ought to go into medicine instead. Insisting on it, in fact, and refusing to help pay for college unless she did it on his terms.

She'd defied her father back then, and she would defy Kai, too. So what if Kai's body called to hers on an elemental level? She refused to be ordered around by any man.

"What gives you the right to tell me what to do?" she demanded.

She put her hands flat on his chest, pushing him right up against the wall. The thatched roof shook, and the whole cottage rattled, but she didn't relent.

"You have no right," she answered before he could. "I don't care if you're a big, bad dragon."

"But—"

She shook her head. "You don't own me. Never tell me where I can go, when, or with whom."

Rage, it seemed, worked well on dragons. Fire fighting fire, maybe, because Kai appeared totally taken aback.

"It could be dangerous out there," he protested. "Last night—"

She couldn't care less about last night or about the hurt-puppy expression on his face. He was the one who'd pissed her off, damn it, and not the other way around.

"You shouldn't leave here without—"

She twisted her hands in his shirt. "Without what? Asking your permission?"

For a minute, he was quiet, and she knew she'd gotten carried away by the temper that flared out of nowhere from time to time. She took a deep breath, trying to calm down. Her nostrils whiffed Kai's scent, and gradually, it dawned on her how close they were. Whoa — very close. Her breasts were pressed up against his chest, and his breath puffed gently on her cheek. His heart thumped under the palm she'd placed against his chest, and something inside her woke up and purred like a cat stretching after a long winter's nap.

She stared into his eyes. Every emotion that had been missing when he'd first appeared had rushed back in, turning the glow from red to a warm, pulsing blue. The light, outermost part of the glow was the tenderness she'd yearned for. The royal blue inner ring was respect. And the darkest flicks of indigo near his pupils — well, that looked a hell of a lot like desire.

Her heart beat a little faster. Did her eyes show all that, too?

His thigh pressed against her hip, too, and damn — there it was again. That heat. That primal call. That blinding need.

She'd had to brace her arms and legs to be able to push that hulk of a man, but as the anger drained out of her, her muscles relaxed one after another, going soft and mushy, like her heart.

Don't, she warned herself. *Don't give this man an inch. He'll take a yard.*

Kai, however, didn't look like he was about to take a yard. His hands caught hers — gently. And in a tiny, barely perceptible movement, his thumbs stroked her skin.

She took a deep breath. Had he really just chased her anger away?

"You can't tell me what to do," she whispered, dipping her chin to avoid his gaze.

That brought her eyes to his chest, which rose and fell with each steady breath. Her chest rose and fell too, and she fought the urge to squeeze closer.

The red filter over her vision softened to a golden glow. The sea breeze stirred the curtains, fanning Kai's scent closer. He smelled of leather, salt, and the wind, and she couldn't help but inhale. There was a little trace of the soap she'd used to clean him off earlier, too, and she warmed at the memory.

His chest filled at the same time, making her blink. Was he sniffing her scent, too?

"Tessa," he whispered. Softly. Hoarsely.

She peeked at his face. Big mistake, because that brought her within an inch of his lips. They were dry but nowhere near as cracked and swollen as before.

"Are you really okay?" she whispered, mesmerized by the swirling fire in his eyes. Was that a dragon trick to entice innocent maidens? She dismissed the thought immediately. Hell, she was no maiden. And part of her longed to be enticed. To be held and cherished the way his eyes promised he would.

"I'm fine. Thanks." He dipped his chin, bringing his lips — lips that begged for a kiss — right into range. His eyes dropped to her mouth, and he bit his lip.

She leaned closer, tilting her head. Zeroing in on the kiss they both yearned for.

"Don't kiss me," he whispered, even hoarser than before. He didn't move, though. Nothing but his lips, forming the words, which only made her blood pump faster.

"You can't tell me what to do," she murmured, low and husky, leaning closer, tightening her grip on his shirt.

One corner of his mouth curled up a tiny bit, but his eyes darkened.

"You really shouldn't kiss me," he said, though his voice gave him away.

"Not even if we both want it?"

"Especially if we both want it."

"You want it. You want to kiss me," she said — not in triumph, but in wonder. She leaned forward, nudging her hips toward his.

"I want more than to kiss you," he rumbled so low she had to strain to hear.

He wants me. Her soul danced.

"But listen," Kai whispered. "I'm a dragon, and you're human..."

She moved her hands over his chest. "What I'm touching feels plenty human to me."

Kai opened his mouth to add something she was sure she didn't want to hear, and time slowed down. Way, way down until every second was a minute and a minute was an eternity.

Kiss him. Kiss your mate, a little voice in the back of her mind urged.

She felt time stretch to its very limits, like a rubber band about to snap. Time or fate or destiny was giving her one last chance to act before Kai blinked and pulled away.

He wants this, the little voice said. *You want this. Kiss him. Seek your destiny. Fight for it.*

Tessa closed her eyes, tipped forward on the balls of her feet, and let her lips close over his. She gripped his shirt before he could pull away. But instead of holding her back, Kai reeled her in.

Kiss me, his body cried. She could feel it in the pressure of his hands over her back, in the thump of his heart. *Please kiss me.*

She let her lips move over his the way the moonlight rippled over the sea at night. Then she slid a hand behind his head, tugging him closer. Telling him how much she wanted that kiss and how right it felt. Whatever resistance Kai had didn't come from his heart or soul. It came from some dark, haunted place she had to free him from.

Kiss me, she cried, wishing she could send her thoughts into his mind.

He opened his mouth, inviting her to taste, to explore. So she did, marveling the whole time. He was so gentle. So hungry. So yielding. Not at all dragon-like, or at least, what she expected of a dragon.

But his arms trembled under hers, and his torso was rock-hard. And suddenly, she understood. He was holding back. Warring with himself — perhaps even warring with his dragon. Proving to her that a dragon shifter didn't have to be bossy and domineering, after all. Not when it counted most.

"Making sure you're not scaring me off?" she whispered into his lips.

"I want you too much to screw this up," he said gruffly.

A little chorus of angels sang in her ears. Her chest swelled, and her heart beat faster as she rubbed against him.

"Just don't stop," she panted a moment later. "And I guarantee you won't screw this up."

His body surged forward, holding her tight. "Don't want to stop."

She wove her hands through his thick, dark hair, and dove into a kiss of a reply. A long, wet kiss that visited every corner of his mouth while her fingers mapped every contour of his shoulders.

It was a kiss that tasted like sunrise and rainbows and all kinds of wondrous, promising things, and she found herself whimpering. Squeezing her body closer to his—

Suddenly, she remembered his injuries and pulled back with a sharp intake of breath. "Are you really okay?"

He cocked his head with a dazed expression that said he'd been as submerged in that kiss as she.

"Fine."

She ran her hands over his shoulders, then over his chest, finding the nub of his nipple. Hadn't he had a long gash there?

She traced his skin gingerly, but all she could find were hard, flat planes of muscle.

"Really fine?"

His shirt was tucked into his jeans, and she tugged the tail out. Slowly, she pulled the fabric upward, revealing smooth, unblemished skin. A hell of a lot of skin, ridged at the six-pack of his abs.

He looked at her, expressionless. Was he afraid she might bolt?

"Shifters heal quickly. See? Perfect."

She gulped. Yeah, he was perfect, all right. Still, she worked his shirt off for further proof. Kai wasn't kidding. It was as if his injuries had never been there — except his right shoulder, because he winced when it moved.

"Okay, except maybe that part," he murmured, reeling her in for another kiss.

Her body heat rose another notch at the sensation of all that hot, hard muscle, and she let her fingers play over the waistband of his jeans. The kiss grew harder. Hungrier. Her blood rushed in her ears as she led him through a turn, until she was the one with her back against the wall and he was the one blocking her in.

"Your turn, mister," she breathed, arching into him.

"You sure?" he murmured.

She nearly laughed. Yes, she was sure. So sure, she was about to yowl and wrap her leg around his.

Kai lifted her right hand until he had it pinned against the wall, followed up with the left, and then she was trapped. Deliciously trapped and wriggling against his body.

"So sure," she murmured, reaching out with her lips.

He kissed her with what felt like his heart, body, and soul. His fingers laced through hers as he ground his groin against her hips at the same measured, insistent pace as his tongue. Tessa found herself surging forward, like he was the shore and she was the wave. Or was it the other way around? She couldn't tell any more. Not with sheer, animal need sweeping over her like never before.

Literally, like never before. As if the couple of men she'd ever slept with were just dreams, and she was experiencing the real thing for the first time.

"So sure," she moaned as Kai dipped lower, claiming her neck in huge, openmouthed kisses that sucked, licked, and burned.

She tipped her head back, giving him free access, then wiggled when he pulled her shirt over her head and unclipped her bra. A second later, he had her pinned again, his mouth on her neck. The world seemed to tip forward slowly until she realized Kai was moving down her body, inch by inch. He kissed the hollow at the bottom of her neck, the delicate line of her collarbone, then the swell of her breast.

"Oh, yes," she whispered, stretching upward until her nipple slid into his mouth.

When Kai sealed his lips over the pink nub and sucked, she nearly squealed.

"Yes," she murmured, giving in to the rush, the high of her dragon.

Her dragon? Was she nuts?

Mine, a deep, growly voice deep in her soul said. *Mate.*

Chapter Eleven

Every time Tessa moaned or writhed under his touch, Kai's dragon roared.

Yes. Please her. Please our mate.

Kai nearly snorted. As if he needed any encouragement.

There, his dragon murmured as her breast swelled under his touch. *She likes that.*

He grumbled, because it wasn't as if he needed instructions, either. He wasn't a kid anymore.

Feels like it's our first time, his dragon cooed. *With Tessa, everything is different. New.*

That, he had to agree with. If whatever he'd done in the past was called sex, this had to have a different name. A long, lyrical Hawaiian name full of joyous vowels that rolled off his tongue.

Roll. Tongue. Good idea, his dragon murmured as Tessa moaned. She was arched so far back, he could easily slide his hands over her back and scoop her closer, accentuating her amazing curves. He turned his head sideways, sucking from below while pushing upward, feeling the full weight of her breasts.

Heaven, his dragon purred. *Heaven.*

His soreness had vanished along with the last of his fears when she'd whispered for more. Deep down, he sensed both would come back with a vengeance later. But right now, his mate needed him. She was begging for him.

He nipped her breast, then soothed it with his tongue, finding it smooth but for the tiny bumps surrounding her nipple. His eyes just about rolled back in his head as he memorized each and every one.

Mate wants me. Mate isn't afraid, his dragon cooed. *Our mate is strong.*

She was strong. Strong and determined. Who'd ever man-handled him against a wall like that? And hell — she had anger down, for sure. A pure, blazing anger that could burn down a barn if she had the power to open her jaws and spit fire.

But her anger had ebbed as quickly as it came, revealing the passionate soul beneath. A soul desperate for love and acceptance, if only on her own terms.

Well, he could do her terms, especially if the reward was *this.*

So good, his dragon moaned, tasting her again and again.

It had been hell holding his dragon back at first, but the beast had quickly settled down and enjoyed the ride, letting his human side maintain control.

Speaking of enjoying the ride. . . his dragon murmured, hinting at the bed.

Soon, Kai told it. *Soon. She calls the shots.*

Tessa's right shoulder dipped, and he responded by switching over to her right breast. He kneaded the left at the same time — kneading and rolling the nipple between his fingers, pinching just hard enough to make her gasp then sigh.

"Yes," she moaned, pushing against him. "Yes. . . "

That word, he wanted to hear a thousand times in the next hour.

Hours. Days. Weeks, his dragon agreed.

The very thought made his cock swell in his jeans. That was already a damn tight fit, but now, it was worse. Every dragon had a healthy sexual appetite, but destined mates were legendary for sealing their eternal bond through marathon sessions that stretched over weeks. Weeks in which no one dared disturb the lovers for fear of a dragon's wrath.

He exhaled against Tessa's skin. Wrath. That would be the word for what he'd show if anyone came between him and his mate.

"Ouch," she squeaked.

102

He rubbed her skin quickly, cursing himself. Shit, he had to be careful. That exhale had come from his dragon side, and it was dangerously close to a puff of fire — the brand dragons used to mark their mates right after exchanging mating bites. A brand that burned briefly while releasing great pleasure, just as the most passionate sex did. Or so he'd heard, because few dragons were blessed with a destined mate — a woman to love for all eternity.

A woman I will please again and again, his dragon growled.

Kai dropped to his knees, kissing her belly button. He spread his hands wide on her hips, taking his time. Tessa needed to understand that he'd never force her or commandeer. She could call the shots, too.

"Take it off," she said, lifting her hands free of her sarong. "Please. Take it off."

He ran his fingers along the edge of the fabric, then flicked the knot at the front, letting it fall away.

Heaven. He was six inches away from heaven.

"Please. Kai," she breathed, guiding him closer. "Touch me."

He ran his hands down her thighs then back up, trying not to rush. Guiding her legs apart, he leaned in slowly, puffing at her belly.

She threaded her fingers through his hair and tugged him closer. Lower.

He kissed her belly while reaching toward her center, seeking her folds. Touching her gently, then harder, while her body responded with shudders of delight.

"Oh," she murmured, going limp against the wall. "Yes. . . "

Electric zings went through his body when he touched her core, and when he leaned forward to taste her, a thousand little lights blinked on and off in his soul.

Mine, his dragon hummed in his head. *My mate.*

He licked harder. Faster. Deeper. Desperate for Tessa to keep up the whimpers of pleasure he could barely hear above the roar in his ears. Desperate to make her feel good.

Cry for me, my mate, his dragon hummed. *Tell me how good it feels.*

She rocked against his hand and mouth, demanding more. He slipped one finger, then two into her, marveling at how tight and slick she was. How hungry for his touch. He started pumping in time to the flicks of his tongue until she was shuddering and crying out his name.

He slowed gradually, unwilling to let it end as Tessa went limp.

This is the first time we make her feel good, his dragon hummed. *Doesn't mean it will be the last.*

No way would it be the last if he had any say in the matter. But what did Tessa think?

"Kai," she murmured, pulling him back up until they were face-to-face. He grinned in satisfaction at her flushed cheeks and the hazy look in eyes.

"Yes, m'lady?" he said, turning on his best dragon manners.

She hummed a little, then nudged him backward. "That was good. Really, really good."

He nodded, forcing himself to meet her eyes instead of admiring the red marks his stubble had rubbed into her thighs and breasts.

Her full, beautiful breasts. His dragon licked his lips.

She caught him by the waistband, popped the button of his jeans, and slid down the fly. "Really good — for me. Time to make it up to you." She slid her hand inside his jeans.

"Okay," he whispered, trying to keep his voice even despite the fireworks exploding in his groin. "Fine."

She cocked an eyebrow in challenge. "Just fine?" She pushed his jeans and boxers down then cupped his balls.

He gulped, forcing himself to stay in control. "How about really good?"

Tessa pressed close to his chest to whisper in his ear. "How about I make it even better?"

Her nipples pressed into his skin, and when she grasped his cock, he sucked in a quick breath.

"Please."

Please, his dragon begged.

"How's that?" She stroked up and down. Every time she reached the tip of his cock and turned around, she tugged the foreskin, making his teeth clench, it felt so good. And every time she reached the base of his cock, she made sure her knuckles grazed his balls.

He wished for something to hang on to, because this woman was about to bring him to his knees. He hung on to her instead, trying not to show how close to coming he was. Probably failing, judging by the naughty expression on her face. But that was okay. This was Tessa. For her, he'd come undone. For her, he'd drop his outer defenses and let her see just how she affected him.

"Let's take these off, shall we?"

When she loosened her grip and helped him step out of his jeans, her eyes widened at the unobstructed sight of him.

She likes what she sees, his dragon crooned.

He'd make damn sure she'd like what she felt when they took things to the next level, too.

She started stroking him again. Stroking and backing him toward the bed, kissing his ear as she went. Exhaling into his neck, driving him wild.

You sure we can't take over yet? his dragon begged.

Not until she says so. Not yet.

It wasn't as if he was suffering, though, and his dragon quickly acquiesced.

"I don't suppose you have a condom in your pocket," she murmured, groping around his thigh in a joke.

He hissed. Shit. There was no way he was going to make it to his place and back sporting a hard-on this size. And there was no way he would leave Tessa at a time like this.

She grinned and pushed him to a sitting position on the bed. "Well, I just happen to have gotten my luggage back today, and guess what I keep in my toiletry bag?"

He laughed, falling back in relief. Thank goodness for that.

The position made his cock jut up obscenely, and Tessa stared. When she licked her lips, he fantasized about her crouching over him and—

She shook herself a little and murmured, "Next time."

Next time was fine with him, as long as there was a next time. And a time after that and after that...

She turned to root around in her suitcase, giving him a full view of her rear. A view that distracted him from the colorful clothes strewn out the sides of her bag and the corner of a little wooden box. Why look at that when he could admire Tessa? She even wiggled a little, making him fantasize about crouching behind her and taking her that way. Hot and hard and on all fours until she came, screaming his name and—

He turned his head away and added another wish to the *next time* list.

"There it is," she murmured, turning back to him with a foil packet in her hand like a prize. She stepped back and stood over him, then held it next to his cock. "Think it will fit?"

"It better fit," he growled, though it seemed pretty damn impossible.

"Well then," she cooed, placing a hand against his chest. "Lie back, relax, and let me do the rest."

He hesitated just long enough for her to tilt her head, making her hair cascade to one side.

A moment of truth, he sensed. Could he really coax his dragon into handing over the reins? Could he prove to her how much she meant to him?

For you, my mate, his dragon hummed.

He lay back on the firm mattress, waiting for her.

Tessa blinked a little, hesitating. It was as novel a position for her as for him, he sensed. Her hand trembled, and her chest heaved.

"Coming, m'lady?" he whispered.

She took a deep breath and stepped right back into power woman mode. "Coming. Coming."

Me, too, he wanted to quip. His cock ached. His heart was beating like a jackhammer, and his eyes burned — a sure sign that they were glowing. That didn't faze Tessa, though. In fact, her eyes seemed to glow, too. Or maybe that was what his dragon wanted to see.

She'd make a good dragon, he couldn't help thinking as she ripped the packet open and unrolled the condom over his cock. He closed his eyes, relishing her touch.

Imagine doing this without the barrier someday, his dragon hummed. *Skin-to-skin.*

Yeah, that would be even better, but he wasn't going to push his luck right now.

"Coming," Tessa murmured, crawling over him.

She jerked her chin, and both of them wiggled up the bed until his head was nestled among the pillows and his body spread on the bed. Her eyes explored every part of his body as she slowly straddled him. They locked eyes, and she lowered herself gradually, drawing out the anticipation. She pressed down a little too high, but that was all part of the fun. Feeling the damp heat between her legs. Seeing her eyes narrow on his.

When Kai placed his hands on her hips and guided her lower, she dragged her body along his, extending that moist trail.

"You, woman, are cruel," he murmured.

"You love it," she countered, playing it cool though her voice was higher than usual.

She dragged up and down along his body, right over his cock. Spreading her legs wider, letting his shaft find the notch between her folds just long enough to tease before sliding away again.

"Torture," he lied as she slid higher again.

Good torture, his dragon agreed.

Her red hair flowed over her shoulders, and her breasts swayed tantalizingly close to his mouth. So close, he considered lifting higher to suckle. But Tessa closed her eyes, getting into the groove as her body responded to his, and he didn't dare break the moment. Instead, he reached around her perfect ass, coaxing her into a wider straddle.

This is going to be so good, his dragon whispered, flicking its tail.

ANNA LOWE

Like he needed an oversized reptile to tell him that. Kai soaked in the sheer beauty of the moment. Tessa's beauty. Her pent-up need. Her determination to get this exactly right.

When she dragged her body higher and rose up on her knees, he held his breath. She moved into position, letting the crest of his cock nestle against her folds, and lowered herself inch by inch.

"Oh," she murmured, tipping her head back.

Her sweet heat enveloped him, and he gritted his teeth. *No pushing up. No forcing anything. Let her adjust,* he ordered his dragon.

Yes, his dragon coaxed. *Let me fill you, my mate.*

"Yes," she hissed, taking another inch of him.

She was so tight. All heat, all muscle inside.

"God, Kai," she whispered, waking every nerve in his body. Her voice was music to his ears.

She started rocking. Rocking and murmuring his name. Arching her back. Pushing harder and harder until it was clear she wanted him to push back.

He gripped her hips and looked into her eyes. Was she ready?

Her emerald eyes sparkled. "Kai," she begged.

He pushed upward, and she gasped, though he barely heard her over the sound of his own deep groan.

"Yes. Tessa."

Chapter Twelve

"Kai," Tessa panted, moving faster.

She'd never had a man seated as deep inside, nor one so big. She'd never, ever felt so good. Hazy, but good, because there was a magical quality to the sensations shooting through her body and mind. Was that a bonus of shifter sex or was it the spark-inducing chemistry between her and Kai?

Whatever the reason, she'd never felt so hot inside, so satisfied yet starving at the same time. Every thick, hot slide set off another wave of ecstasy. His grip on her hips was so tight, it hurt — in a good way. It felt as if he never wanted to let her go.

She rocked harder, pushing her hair behind her shoulders, though it just came cascading right back. Kai seemed to like that, though, so she did it again.

"Yes... yes..." She couldn't help murmuring with every little buck. She couldn't help touching herself, either, running her hands over her breasts, teasing her own nipples the way Kai had done.

The glow in Kai's eyes intensified. Yeah, he liked that, all right. So she kept it up, smoothing her skin, squeezing her breasts. Ratcheting up the spiral of energy within.

"So good," she hummed, moving her hands and hips at the same time.

"So beautiful," Kai whispered.

As she adjusted to his size, her body screamed for more. She leaned back, changing the angle, and immediately groaned.

"God, Kai..."

She leaned farther back, seeking more friction, more heat, and Kai's eyes flared each time. She tilted even more, propping her arms against his thighs. Her head lolled from side to side, tipping until she couldn't see Kai anymore. She felt his eyes on her, though. They danced over her breasts, leaving a warm, laser trail there, then moved over her belly toward the point of their connection, where he watched himself slide in and out.

"Kai," she cried, so close to coming, she could barely see straight.

He spread his fingers and dragged his thumb toward her clit, pushing her closer and closer to the edge. He circled her, then pressed the nub.

"Yes..." Up to that point, she'd been moving in a steady rhythm, but her fine motor control disappeared along with the last of her inhibitions, and the motion became more and more desperate. Jerky.

"So close," she panted. Jesus, she was so, so close. But somehow, her body refused to let go. It hung on and on, letting her orgasm build.

She tipped far enough forward to peek at Kai. Why wasn't her body letting her come? What was she doing wrong?

His eyes sparked and flared, but still, he let her lead.

A prince, she almost said. *You are a prince.*

He'd proven she didn't have to fear him ordering her around. And suddenly, just as much as she'd wanted to claim the power position earlier, she was desperate to give it up. She wanted Kai above her, powering in. Hammering, even — harder than she could manage on her own.

After three more jerky bucks, she flopped forward, lying over him.

"Please," she begged — yes, begged — and tipped her body to signal the switch. "Please, Kai."

He slid his hands up to her waist and hesitated. "You sure? You're doing great."

She smiled. The man was truly a prince. A prince she wanted driving into her again and again.

"I want you on top. Need you on top," she insisted. "Need you deeper."

Harder. Faster, she nearly added, along with a whole string of dirty words she'd never considered using before but which felt exactly right at this moment in time. She wanted dirty. She wanted desperate. She wanted to come undone.

Kai held her gaze then nodded slightly. "Hang on."

She'd nearly laughed off the warning — as if she needed to be told that. But, holy cow — the man meant what he said, because when he rolled, putting her back against the mattress, his cock hammered home, making her cry out.

He paused, and she saw lightning in his eyes.

"Keep going," she whispered. "Please don't stop."

It hurt so good, she welcomed the pain.

When Kai pulled back then thrust back in, her vision flashed white before she could focus again — just in time for Kai to pull back again. Back, back, back, making her ache.

Don't go! her body cried. *Don't go!*

But he wasn't pulling out; he was just preparing for an even harder thrust. And the second it came, she moaned. So loud, she pulled a pillow closer to muffle the sound.

"Not too hard?" he asked.

Her legs were wrapped around his waist, and she lifted them higher, spurring him on with her heels. "I want hard. Dragon-hard."

The blue of his eyes blazed, giving her a hint of the beast within.

I will do anything you wish, she imagined the dragon whispering. *I will worship you for the rest of my life.*

She was probably just imagining that, but hell — her body was high on the best drug of all. It wasn't her fault she couldn't see straight.

He pumped back in, and she unleashed her cries into the pillow. Kai's eyes grew brighter, his face fiercer with each successive thrust. Faster, too, until his rhythm became just as jerky as hers had before.

"Tessa. Tessa," he grunted, slipping out of control.

Sweat glistened on his brow and chest, and the drop that fell to her chest might as well have been lava, the way it sizzled on her skin.

"Yes... Yes..."

The ache inside her grew and grew, and this time, she felt herself tipping right over the edge.

"Kai," she cried, spasming around him.

He pumped again — Two times? Three? — then went stiff all over and released inside her with a low groan.

Tessa tipped her head back and closed her eyes, hanging on to the high. Kai's shoulders were rock-hard under her hands, and his ass was immobile under her heels. But he might as well have still been thrusting inside her given the way her body shuddered again and again.

She mumbled. Cried. Pleaded with her body to let her ride that wave of ecstasy a little bit longer.

"Tessa," Kai whispered, dropping down over her.

His body pinned her in place, but even that felt good. She arched against him through another two aftershocks of pleasure, then slowly melted away.

Surely, the games she'd played with other men didn't count as sex. Surely, she'd been doing something wrong in the past. Well, she sure got it right this time. She and Kai both.

"Amazing," Kai murmured, kissing her hair.

She hugged him fiercely, arms and legs reaching as far as they could to wrap him in an embrace, and listened to Kai pant.

"Good for you, too?" she whispered, needing to know it wasn't just her who'd felt the earthquake.

He huffed into her ear. "Are you kidding? Great."

She laughed out loud, and he chuckled, too.

"Thank you," she murmured, kissing his ear. "Thank you."

All the confidence that had left her after the attack in Arizona poured back into her soul. The backbone she was worried she'd never find again. And trust — the most precious gift of all. She could trust Kai. Not just with her body, she sensed. With more. A lot more.

He shook his head. "Thank you."

He rolled to his side and scooped her into his arms, stroking her hair while murmuring those two words again and again.

Tessa closed her eyes and let herself drift on a velvety cloud of bliss. Had she really been mad at Kai a short time back?

Had she really doubted him? She couldn't remember why any more. Only that her fears had all been illusions. Her doubts, unfounded. Her hopes, confirmed.

"Just a second," he said eventually, peeling away. "I need to get rid of this."

She didn't want to let him go, but he had to dispose of the condom, so she released her grip and rolled onto the warm spot he'd left, lying on her stomach like a turtle on a beach.

"Hmm," he said, coming back. "You're giving me bad ideas."

She smiled into the sheets. "Great minds think alike."

He touched her back and combed her hair with his fingers. "Just give me a minute to admire you first."

She sighed with pleasure at his touch. Seconds ago, he'd been all power, all raging force. Now he was gentle and soft.

"Mmm," she hummed as he started massaging her back.

He brushed her hair to one side and kneaded her right shoulder.

"Oh, my God. Heaven," she sighed.

He chuckled then moved to the other side, rearranging her hair to continue. His hands moved smoothly, then abruptly stopped.

She waited a moment then lifted her head from the pillow. "Okay?"

He massaged her shoulders in a rush. "Yeah. Sure."

So why was his voice an octave lower? Why were his movements suddenly sloppier than before?

"Sorry," he murmured, evening out again. "I thought I heard something for a second."

She tipped her head. "I didn't hear anything."

"Probably nothing," he said gruffly.

His hands worked their magic again, and she went back to that blissful, boneless state beneath him, purring like a cat.

He stopped long enough to sweep a thumb over one spot low on her right shoulder. "Have you always had this?"

Her mind was so hazy, a minute ticked by before she understood what he meant. The birthmark her grandmother had tried making her feel better about by calling it a secret gift.

"Yeah. I have another one down there," she sighed, bending her leg to show him the one on her calf.

Kai didn't seem too interested, though. Only on the one on her back. "Sorry. I thought it was a burn at first."

She chuckled, feeling drunk from all the endorphins coursing through her body. "I never burn. Didn't I tell you?"

"Oh, right," he murmured, touching the birthmark gently.

If he'd kept that up a minute longer, she might have wondered why, but then his voice went all smooth and soft, and his hands turned her to putty again.

He worked his way down her back. So low, she started to spread her legs in hopes of Kai touching her more intimately again. But he slowly worked his way up her body, and after one final kiss on the back of her neck, he sat up.

"Listen, I need to check in with Silas."

She groaned. "You've spoiled me already. Now I want to chain you to this bed."

He leaned in and whispered into her ear, so low and rumbly, her body shuddered with need. "You won't need chains, Tessa." Then he kissed her once more and stood up. "I'll be back as soon as I can. And, um — well, I'd say, get some rest, but you'd probably get mad at me again. Not that I'd mind if the same thing happened..."

"I'm sorry," she sighed. "How about we try it without the angry part next time?"

"Next time, for sure," he promised.

Turning her head, she watched as he retrieved his clothes and pulled them on again. First his pants, then his shirt. She sighed inside. A damn shame, covering all that skin up again. But if she got a next time, she supposed she shouldn't complain.

"See you soon?" she whispered, trying not to sound too needy.

He crouched in front of her and kissed her forehead, then touched her nose with a finger. "As soon as I can." When he stood, his eyes slid sideways, to some point on her back, but then he yanked them back to her face. "As soon as I can."

Chapter Thirteen

Kai forced himself to walk, not rush, out of the guest cottage. He desperately wanted to stay and spend another hour — another day, or even better, a year — wrapped around Tessa, but his mind spun with what he'd seen. If that birthmark was what he thought, it changed everything. Everything.

He speed-walked up the path, swatting low-hanging branches and palm fronds out of the way. He nearly swatted Boone, too, when the wolf came sauntering along, sniffing deeply and blocking Kai's way.

"Ooh, la la. Someone feels better, I see." The wolf had the good sense to dodge Kai's arm and step aside before he was bowled over, though. "What's the hurry?"

"Have you seen Silas?"

Boone laughed. "Never seen a man in such a hurry to leave his mate for a grouch like Silas."

Kai stopped in his tracks and spun. "What did you just say?"

Boone shrugged. "Come on, we all know Silas is a grouch, so—"

"Not that part."

Boone cracked into a wry grin. "Ah. The part about your mate."

"How the hell do you know that?"

"It's obvious, man. Your eyes glow every time you look at her. Not the angry glow. The glow Silas used to have when..." Boone trailed off, and they stood in awkward silence, eyeing the path up to Silas's house. "Anyway," Boone continued a second later. "It was obvious the second you brought Tessa here. Don't tell me you're still kidding yourself about that, are you?"

Kai took a deep breath. No, he wasn't kidding himself anymore. Tessa was his destined mate. And yes, his soul had told him as much the moment they'd met, but he'd been trying to deny the attraction for her own good.

"Like you'd be any different," he scowled at Boone.

The wolf shifter laughed out loud. "Me, I'd know my mate the second I met her. Except, of course, I never will." For a moment, his jaunty tone broke and his eyes dimmed. But then he grinned, playing the jokester again. Good old Boone, master of hiding from emotions he didn't want to face. "So, you and Tessa finally—"

Kai cut him off with a growl. "I need to talk to Silas. Right now."

"Yeah, well. Good luck convincing him, man."

Kai clenched his teeth and strode up the steep path toward Silas's place. Like his, it stood high on a rocky cliff overlooking the sea. But while Kai's place was all clean angles and open space, Silas's house was all arches and curves. The house belonged to the owner of the estate, who'd had the place built by some up-and-coming architect specializing in open-design masterpieces made entirely of bamboo — as in, three-story treehouse style, a cross between the Sydney Opera House and something out of the Jungle Book. Since the reclusive estate owner was never around, Silas lived in one wing.

A stream gurgled, paralleling the path Kai followed as his stomach knotted with emotions. He'd never really believed he'd find a mate, and damn, he was practically bumping into things out of sheer joy. Joy and terror, because what if something happened to Tessa? Or worse, what if she rejected him?

Mate loves us, his dragon assured him. *She knows who we are.*

He clenched his fists. Would that change when he confronted her with the truth? Could she handle finding out who — and what — *she* really was?

The last few steps, he took two at a time, climbing briskly until he stepped onto the lowest patio of the place. No need to call out for Silas, because his cousin was already there, arms crossed, scowling.

Kai folded his arms and scowled back, hiding his instinctive gulp.

"I tell you to learn more about that human, and you disappear with her for most of yesterday. I tell you to investigate her background, and instead, you go flying all night, and nearly get yourself killed." Silas started pacing around Kai. "I tell you to—" He came to an abrupt halt by Kai's shoulder and sniffed. "You smell like her. Damn it, what have you done?"

Kai gritted his teeth. It had to be crystal clear what he'd done. He hadn't showered after leaving Tessa — and even a shower probably wouldn't have washed off the scent of sex. Not after the way he'd marked her body as his. All that nuzzling was instinctive, as his inner dragon marked Tessa as off-limits to any other man.

"Listen, Silas—"

"No, you listen to me," Silas barked. "We agreed to help because Ella asked us. We agreed to keep Tessa safe — but not for any longer than necessary. You know the rules. Damn it, you helped make those rules. No humans."

"What's more important — some rule or destiny?"

"Destiny?" Silas's voice filled with scorn. "You think she's your mate?"

"I know she is."

Silas stepped closer, his eyes blazing. "The stories we were raised with were a bunch of lies. Destiny isn't benevolent, Kai. Destiny is cruel, playing games with our hearts. With our souls." His voice filled with the anger and pain he usually kept simmering beneath the surface.

"What happened to you wasn't a trick of destiny, Si—"

His cousin shoved him and prowled closer. "This isn't about me. It's about you. Destiny fucked with your parents. Now it's fucking with you. You know the risks of taking a human mate."

"She's not human. Not entirely," Kai cut in.

Silas jerked to a halt. "What?"

"You were right about why Morgan wants her."

"She's a fire maiden? How can you be sure?"

Kai shook his head. "Not just a fire maiden. She's part dragon. She carries the brand, Silas. The brand of the Baird Clan."

Silas went still at the mention of the legendary dragon clan. "Are you sure?"

Kai nodded slowly. "It's just like the stories say." He made a butterfly shape with his fingers. "This big. Right here, on her back." He motioned over his own shoulder.

"A descendant of the house of Baird," Silas whispered. "You're absolutely sure?"

Kai nodded, and for a moment, the only sound was that of the wind whispering through the trees.

Silas studied him from head to toe. "Could just be a birth-mark."

Kai scoffed.

"All right, if she's a fire maiden — and not just any fire maiden, but one descended from the house of Baird — every dragon ought to be after her. Desperately."

Kai tilted his head. What was Silas getting at?

"I didn't feel a thing," Silas said, crossing his arms over his chest.

Kai snorted. "You haven't felt a thing for years. Ever since Moira—"

Silas cut him off. "Don't."

Kai didn't know exactly what had happened between Silas and the dragon female he'd been betrothed to. Only that it had ended badly. But, damn it, he had to get the truth into his cousin's thick head. "You still love Moira, don't you?"

Silas's eyes swirled red, and a growl rose from his throat.

Kai went on nonetheless. "Fine. Keep pretending whatever happened didn't happen and that it didn't affect you. But don't let it keep me from claiming my mate."

"Moira has nothing to do with this."

Kai went on, undeterred. "You still love Moira."

"Of course, I still—" Silas started, then cut himself off, aware of what he'd just admitted.

Kai pressed on. "That kept you from being attracted to Tessa. But I noticed her from the very start."

Silas stepped forward. "Fine. So you're attracted to Tessa. Like I said, destiny plays games. Morgan wants her, too. Does that make her his fated mate?"

Kai looked at his feet. Shit. Was his interest in Tessa purely physical?

No! his dragon roared, giving him a thousand other reasons to love Tessa. Reasons Kai struggled to put into words.

"I'd never force her. I'd never lock her up," he started.

Silas shrugged, unconvinced.

"I feel her moods. Even from a distance."

Silas huffed. "I swear, when that woman gets mad, everyone on Maui can feel it."

Kai felt his face contort in something between a grin and a scowl. Tessa sure did have a temper — deeply buried, but when it was ignited...

Very dragon-like, his inner beast hummed.

"Can you feel it when she's happy?" he asked Silas. "Do you want to *make* her happy? Do you go to sleep wondering what you can do to make her smile the next morning, or how many times you can make her smile?"

Silas raised his eyebrows. A long, thoughtful moment later, he nodded softly. "Maybe you really do love her."

Hearing someone else say it made Kai pause. Wow. Did he really mean all those things? He thought back over the past few days and decided, yes. Absolutely. Yes, he did.

"Tessa may have dragon blood, but I love her for her. She's my destined mate."

His shoulders lifted as if a weight had been taken from him. A weight he'd put there himself and only now shed.

Silas pursed his lips. "Well, if she does have dragon blood, it's no wonder Morgan wanted her."

Kai growled. "He's not getting her."

Silas gave a curt nod. "You're right. We can't let him have her. We need her."

Kai stepped forward, glowering. "Quit that. Tessa's not a thing, Silas. She's a woman. Her own person."

"I know that. You know that. But Morgan sees her as a treasure — the kind of treasure he would kill for. Morgan, and enemies far more powerful than him."

Kai showed his teeth. "Let them try to take her."

Silas made a face. "They already did. Twice."

Kai winced. Morgan had already locked Tessa up in Phoenix. If Ella hadn't rescued her, Tessa would still be Morgan's prisoner. The thought made Kai sick. He would have gone on with his life not even knowing his destined mate was out there — not knowing she needed his help. And Christ, Tessa would be living in hell. Morgan would force himself on her and—

Kai swallowed hard and forced the horrifying images away. No way would he allow anything to happen to Tessa. No way.

"Last night shows that he's moving in," Silas muttered.

"Let him move in," Kai snarled. "I'll kill him the way I killed those no-good scouts of his."

Silas threw up his hands. "What if Morgan comes with double the help? Trained warriors, not a couple of scouts. Are you going to take on a whole army by yourself?"

Kai worked his jaw. Yes, he'd take on a whole army if he had to. But Silas was right. If he was outnumbered by stronger foes, one little mistake could cost him everything. It would cost Tessa everything, too.

"By myself, huh?" He glowered at his cousin. His whole life, he'd been taught that he had to stick to what little family he had. Silas had said it a hundred times. Was Silas really going to leave him on his own now?

Silas thumped Kai's shoulder. "I'm with you, you idiot. Of course, I'm with you. But even the two of us — plus the others — may not be enough."

"You really think Morgan has that much power? He's rich, but he's not Drax."

Silas grimaced. "No, he isn't. You'd better hope Drax doesn't know about Tessa."

Kai scraped the flagstone underfoot, making a low, screeching sound.

"I'll kill Drax, too."

Silas's hand tightened on his shoulder. "No one wants to kill Drax more than me. But we're not ready to take him on, Kai. Not yet."

"So if Drax comes after Tessa, we let her go?" He glared at Silas, letting the fury show in his eyes.

Silas stretched to his full height, reminding Kai who was the bigger man — and dragon — if only by a hair.

"If it's Drax, we have bigger problems than one woman."

"My mate," Kai growled. "My mate. You should know what that feels like, Silas. If it were Moira—"

"Don't." Silas cut him off with a low, murderous growl. "Don't."

Kai hardly cared. If rubbing that old wound with salt was what it took to convince Silas, so be it. All he cared about was protecting Tessa.

"I can't let her go. I won't let her go. If it were your mate, you'd feel the same."

"If it were my mate. . . " Silas broke off with a pained huff, glaring at Kai.

The air practically crackled with tension as the two men glowered at each other. Then a bird rustled through the trees, and Silas shook his head. "We need to think this through." He took a deep breath and fell into one of his thoughtful silences.

Kai started pacing around the patio, cursing Morgan. If the dragon really was allied with Drax. . . Part of him simply wanted to hope Morgan was acting alone, but no good soldier operated on hope. He needed a plan.

"Does Tessa know?" Silas's voice sliced into the tense silence.

"Know what?"

Silas waved his hands in exasperation. "Know that you're mates."

Kai wrung his hands together. "We only just. . . "

Silas scoffed. "You only just fucked her, and you're convinced—"

Time stopped, and everything in Kai's vision went red. Everything around him became a blurry rush. There was a roaring sound, a crash, a slam, and—

121

Time ticked into motion again, and, shit, he realized he'd just flung Silas back against the stone retaining wall and grabbed him by the throat. Kai's dragon teeth were extending, and his eyes burned — a sure sign they were glowing in rage.

"Do. Not. Say. That. About. My. Mate." He growled each word into Silas's face, absolutely, positively ready to take his cousin on.

Silas's eyes sparked and his body tensed under Kai's firm hold. But a second later, the orange hue faded to yellow, and Silas nodded once.

"You mean it. She is your mate."

"Of course, I mean it." Kai pushed away.

Of course, we mean it, his dragon grumbled inside.

Silas scowled and glanced at his watch. "I have to catch a flight to Oahu to see if I can track down the dragon who got away. You, meanwhile, think carefully. Think it through. I mean, without leapfrogging to whatever damn happily-ever-after your dragon wants to skip ahead to."

Right on cue, Kai's dragon sighed, picturing curling up around Tessa. Tessa with a sleepy, green-eyed baby in her arms.

Kai stood perfectly still before he was bowled over by the onslaught of emotion that image aroused in him.

"Even if she does have dragon blood, she doesn't know what it means to be mates," Silas said. "She doesn't know what it means for her. What she's risking. Or did you explain?" Silas arched a doubtful eyebrow.

Kai kicked the ground. No, he hadn't explained. He hadn't had a chance.

"Didn't think so," Silas muttered. "You need to claim her as soon as you can. Make her your mate so no one else can take her."

Kai looked at the sky. Sure. He'd run right back to Tessa and say, *I need to screw you again right now. And when we're done, I need to bite your neck and breathe fire into the wound. But don't worry — I hear it feels great. And that way you'll be stuck with me forever, and no other dragon can take you away.*

Dragons mated for life, and when one partner died, the other followed shortly after. Even if Morgan killed Kai, he couldn't force Tessa to bond with him — not once she'd given herself to another man.

But he didn't want Tessa to *have* to mate with him. He wanted her to want it as desperately as he did. To dream about it. To make the occasion the beautiful memory it deserved to be — not a business arrangement, a do-or-die.

He could just see Silas butting in and trying to explain to Tessa. *I need you to mate with Kai. For your own good. Oh, and dragon numbers are down, so please bear as many offspring as you can.*

Yeah, right. He could see her reaction already — Tessa with both hands on her hips, lips in a tight, angry line. No way was he going to convince her to mate with him that quickly. He needed time to win her over. To answer her questions. To put her at ease.

But, shit. He didn't have time. The enemy was already closing in, plotting to take Tessa away.

Chapter Fourteen

Tessa reluctantly rose and stretched, wondering how long Kai would be away. She was dying for more time with him — and to ask about how he'd sustained his injuries. She hadn't gotten around to asking earlier because of the way one thing had led to another and. . .

She snorted. One thing had led to another, like her naked on top of him in bed.

Just thinking about it made her body warm up and want to roll in the sheets.

But she wasn't about to lounge around naked, waiting for a man. So she took a lazy shower, running her hands over all the spots he'd touched. Which made for a heck of a lot of spots and a heck of a long shower. The bathroom was steaming when she emerged, and when she wrapped a towel around herself and stepped toward her suitcase, a cloud of mist followed her.

She knelt to sort through her clothes, only then remembering her grandmother's box. And whoa — if that wasn't a sign that Kai had totally blanked out her mind, she didn't know what was. How could she forget what she'd found in the box? She sat on the bed, holding the box, reading the note folded inside.

My dearest Tessa, the note began. A note written on brittle, time-worn paper. *What my grandmother gave to me so long ago, I now give to you.*

Tessa ruffled her fingers through the cloth buffer in the box and gingerly took out the gemstone hidden within.

The stone I gave you years ago was a placeholder for this one — the real thing.

Tessa tilted the emerald, and the sun blazed through it, carrying a beam of green light across the room.

"Grandma," she whispered, unable to fathom it all. The emerald was exactly the size and shape of her pendant but much heavier, like a solid chunk of glass.

Her grandmother had barely made ends meet. And yet, she'd hung on to the precious stone for decades, refusing to part with it. Why?

Her hand shook as she read on. *Now you are the guardian of this great gift from our ancestors.*

She looked at the stone, wondering who those ancestors might be.

Perhaps it will reawaken the way the legends say. Perhaps it will slumber, waiting for the next generation.

Tessa studied the gem. What legends? And why did her grandmother describe the emerald as if it were a living, breathing thing?

Either way, it is your job to keep it safe. Keep it in the family. If you do so, it, too, will keep you safe.

She rubbed the goose bumps that broke out on her arms. Safe? Did her grandmother mean safe against men like Damien Morgan? But what could a stone possibly do?

Trust me, my daughter's daughter. Trust those who have come before you, and trust your heart.

Her heart beat faster as she read on, holding her breath.

May you live and prosper and feel joy as I have, my beloved granddaughter. May the powers in you guide you well.

Tessa gulped and turned the paper over, only to find the back blank. That was it?

She searched for a postscript, then held the note up to the light, hoping some faint letters might appear — but there was nothing. She searched the box and reread the note. Couldn't her grandmother have been a little more specific?

Tessa studied the looping script. Handwriting changed as a person aged, but she was sure her grandmother didn't use quite as flowery a script. She held the emerald up again, turning it so that the light bounced off one edge then another, sending beams of pure green light off at different angles each time.

Then it hit her. Her grandmother's name was Theresa — Tessa, like her. And her grandmother's grandmother was named Tessa, too.

"Holy. . . " She sniffed the paper. Maybe the stone wasn't the only hand-me-down. Maybe the note had been passed through the generations as well.

She held very still, considering the implications. What if the true meaning of those words had been lost with time? Her grandmother might have been as confused as Tessa was now. Maybe she hadn't explained because she didn't know how to explain.

The emerald was strung on a silver chain, and Tessa slowly slipped it over her neck, just for the feel of it. The gem had to be worth a fortune. What was she going to do with it?

Take care of this well, she remembered her grandmother saying when she'd first given her the pendant, years ago. *Show me how responsible you can be.*

Had her grandmother been quietly preparing her all along?

Tessa huffed in frustration. If her grandmother had been preparing her, why hadn't she explained anything?

Trust me, the note said. *Trust those who have come before you, and trust your heart.*

The bushes rustled outside, and Tessa locked her hand over the stone, hiding it. When no further sound came, she dressed quickly. That sound might not have signaled danger, but she couldn't sit around in a wet towel all day.

As she rooted through the suitcase for some underwear, she came across the cell phone she'd packed in in her hurry to flee Arizona. She held it for a moment, wondering if she should turn it on. Hawaii felt a million miles away from the mainland and Damien Morgan. Did she really want to check in on that world?

She hesitated a moment longer, then turned it on. It took an eternity to find a connection, but then it beeped, and dozens of messages appeared on the screen — many marked *urgent.* She winced, recognizing the numbers of clients. Clients she'd stood up when she left Arizona unexpectedly. She sat down

127

hard. All the work she'd put into building her business could be ruined.

There were so many messages, she didn't know where to start. She scrolled through them hopelessly until a message from a number that wouldn't display caught her attention.

She tapped on the message, skim read, then stopped and read again as a cold sensation crept down her spine.

Urgent. Need to talk to you right away, the message said. *You may not be safe. I fear there is a traitor among our friends.* *—Ella*

Tessa stood and listened intently to the sounds outside. Ella had told her she'd be safe at Koa Point. Tessa checked the message time stamp — only a few hours old. Did Ella find out something she wasn't aware of before?

There was a second message that went on in the same vein.

I hope to God you read this in time. Get out. Don't tell anyone where you've gone. I'm coming to help. But I can't come too close. Meet me at Kaunolu...

Tessa skimmed the instructions below, then balked. Kaunolu was on a whole separate island — Lanai. She looked out the front door and over the sea to the pyramid of land to the west.

There's a ferry there a couple of times a day, Kai had said that day they'd driven through town.

There's a ferry... Ella's message echoed, detailing where Tessa should go and when.

Tessa's pulse raced as she peered across the estate — what she could see of it, at least. Was Boone the traitor? That was hard to believe. Hunter struck her as loyal as a bear could be. But Cruz... She froze. Cruz had always been testy around her. On the other hand, he'd been pretty open in his distaste. Wouldn't a traitor hide his true feelings better than that?

She gasped, wondering if it could be Silas. Kai was with Silas at that very moment. Panic seized her when she thought about how long Kai had been away. Hadn't he said he'd be right back?

He'd been injured the night before — from a fight, not just a crash. Which might mean that Kai had already confronted the traitor and triumphed. Which could mean that everything was all right.

But, shit. The shiver in her spine sure didn't give her the feeling everything was all right.

The emerald bit into her palm as she squeezed unconsciously, and she unlocked her grasp. Did the emerald have anything to do with Ella's warning? But how could it?

None of it made sense, but the longer she waited, the likelier it would be that. . . that. . .

She struggled to fill in the blank. That, what? What might happen?

A shadow danced across the doorway, and she remembered Damien Morgan jumping at her. Pinning her against the wall and grunting horrifying messages in her ear.

You will make me a good mate. You will breed me many heirs, and I will become the most powerful of my kind.

Her heart raced long after she realized the movement outside was just a palm dancing in the wind.

A moment later, she grabbed her backpack, stuffed the top couple of items from her suitcase in, and peeked out the door. Kai was a big boy. He'd healed quickly from his injuries, and she could scarcely imagine a foe that could threaten him. The best course of action was to follow Ella's instructions and find out what was going on. She could call Kai once she had a clearer idea of the situation. She didn't have his number, but that wouldn't be hard to find out, right?

Just in case, she scribbled a note on a scrap of paper and hid it under the pillow. If anyone would look there, it would be Kai, and she was careful not to mention any details. Then she inched out the door, eyeing the shadows, walking slowly so as not to make any noise. She made a big loop around the *akule hale*, avoiding the others and jumping at every scratch in the leaves.

Cruz. It had to be Cruz, right? But, shit. He was a tiger. What were the chances of sneaking around him?

She didn't bump into Cruz, thank God, and none of the others, either. The lush lawns of the estate were all separated by thick brush and trees, allowing her to move stealthily along.

So stealthily, she wondered if that was what it felt like to be a wolf or a bear — or a tiger — slinking along. Dragons, she couldn't imagine slinking, though. Just gliding soundlessly overhead.

She whipped her head up in alarm, but the light beat of wings were those of a bird. On instinct, her fingers closed around the pendant and emerald, the two necklaces intertwined and hiding under the collar of her shirt.

The garage wasn't far away, and she could hear the hum of someone at work. Hunter? Whoever it was, he didn't notice her quiet steps. Tessa rushed the rest of the way to the gate and stared at it for a moment. Shoot. She'd probably trip an alarm if she opened it. She followed the thick bushes to the left until she found a place where the stone wall was low enough to scale. With a soft grunt, she hauled herself over then jogged up to the road.

She looked right then left, stuck out her thumb, and started race-walking along.

The first car passed without pausing, but the second — with a friendly woman driver, to Tessa's relief — stopped immediately and brought her right to the green shack of a ticket office at the ferry dock in town.

"One to Lanai," the woman at the counter said, sliding Tessa a ticket. "Boarding in twenty minutes."

Tessa chewed her lip and fiddled with her phone, rereading Ella's instructions between anxious peeks at the road. Had Kai noticed she was gone yet? Had he found her note? She twisted the hem of her shirt in her hands, hating the possibility that Kai might think she'd left him. She never wanted to leave him.

The thought made her stand very still. Did she really mean that?

Well, yes. Yes, she did. And the second she had a chance to talk to Kai, she'd lay it all on the line. Whatever issue there might be between dragons and humans, she was willing to figure out. If Kai felt the same way. If everything worked out.

If, if, if.

Waiting was torture, even once she boarded the ferry and felt it lurch away from the dock. The sea wasn't rough, but her stomach still tossed and turned.

Trust your heart, the note from her grandmother had said.

Her heart, though, was telling her to turn around and run back to Kai. But it was too late, and Ella's message stuck in her mind.

You may not be safe. I fear there is a traitor among our friends.

It made her shiver, and the air conditioning in the ferry's main cabin didn't help, either. She headed out to the top deck, where the wind tugged her hair, making it fly this way and that.

"Bye-bye, Maui!" a tourist laughed, taking a picture.

Tessa hugged herself. Bye-bye to the feeling of peace and security she'd enjoyed for the last couple of days. The farther she traveled from Kai, the more ominous the world felt until she was just as fearful as she'd been on her flight from Phoenix. Worse, in a way, because she wasn't sure where danger lay any more. Behind her? Ahead?

"Look at the little island, sweetie," a woman said to her son. "Molokini."

Tessa looked, too. Anything to take her mind off the mess of her life. She followed the woman's hand to a sliver of an island to the south.

"Mokonini," the boy echoed. "Why aren't there any houses?"

"It's a preserve. No one is allowed to live there," the mother said.

Sounds perfect, Tessa thought. A place to get away from everyone and everything. Except she wouldn't even be safe there — not from dragons, anyway.

"It used to be a round volcano, but it erupted, and now there's just a crescent left," the mom said.

Her son filled in volcanic sound effects. "Ka-boom! Lots of fire!"

Tessa stepped over to the opposite side of the deck.

131

The water grew rougher, and the clouds clustered over West Maui's peaks darkened.

"Getting closer now," a man commented to his partner, pointing to Lanai.

Getting farther and farther away, Tessa's soul cried as she looked back, trying to make out Koa Point.

She knotted her fingers together, twisting them this way and that. She already missed Kai. So much, it went beyond emotion to the physical. Like a part of her own soul had been taken away.

She looked at her feet. Was it really possible to fall in love so fast? Was there really such a thing as destined mates? Her grandmother used to talk about soul mates. Was that the same thing?

The first part of the ferry ride seemed to take forever, but the second half went too quickly because suddenly, she didn't feel so sure about going to Lanai any more. As green and lush as Maui was, Lanai looked browner, more barren. Thornier, if that was the word. A broken line of cliffs slid by as the ferry motored closer, giving the impression of a hostile, savage place.

Tessa squirmed in her seat and felt for the emerald she'd looped around her neck along with the copy she'd carried for so many years. Maybe she should try to contact Kai. Maybe she should rethink this. But Ella was the one who helped her flee Phoenix safely. And if Ella had come all the way out to Hawaii, it had to be serious, right?

"Come on, honey. Lighten up. This is Hawaii," a middle-aged tourist in a bright Hawaiian shirt said.

"Oh, my gosh," his partner squeaked. "Let me guess. You're a runaway bride."

Tessa gaped. A runaway what?

"Did you get cold feet?" the woman went on.

"Um. . . " Tessa searched for words. No, she wasn't a runaway bride. She didn't have a fiancé. She'd been on her own for years. . . until the past few days when Kai had come into her life.

Kai. Could she really share a future with him?

"Not running away," she murmured, touching the lump of the emerald. Well, not from Kai. But she couldn't exactly say, *Actually, I'm running away from a dragon in Arizona* or, *There's a traitor among the shifters of Koa Point, and I'm running away from him. I think it might be the tiger.*

She looked at the woman and pursed her lips. Nope. She was definitely not sharing the truth.

Luckily, a mighty splash appeared off the starboard side of the ferry, making the woman and her partner scramble away.

"Whale! Whale!"

It wasn't a whale, as it turned out, but it was enough of a diversion for Tessa to slip back inside. But not for long because the ferry's engines slowed, and a breakwater came into view.

"Ladies and gentlemen, welcome to Lanai," the captain announced over the PA.

Tessa bit her lip.

"Please remain seated until the boat is docked. . . "

The ferry eased past a couple of pleasure boats and bumped the dock. Tessa shouldered her backpack and filed out with the rest of the passengers, turning left past the green-roofed waiting area just as Ella had instructed. And just as Ella's message had said, a green Jeep with a yellow rental sticker on the bumper stood parked at the end.

The keys will be under the rear right mat. . .

Tessa fished around then fingered the keys. Why didn't Ella meet her at the dock? Why all the secrecy?

She looked around. If she was in danger, Ella could be in danger, too. That would explain why Ella insisted in a remote meeting place. Or maybe it was a fox thing. Ella had even said that of Arizona as she waited with Tessa at the airport.

I love the space, the open range.

Tessa looked around. A little island in the Pacific wasn't exactly open range, but Lanai sure did seem sleepy, and the coast the ferry had passed was completely undeveloped. So, yes. It fit in a way.

Tessa found a marked map in the glove compartment and studied it, then slipped into the driver's seat and straightened her shoulders. It was about time she took things into her own hands. She'd been depending on Kai too much for her own good. She had to orient herself to the area, fast.

It was midweek and late afternoon, when more passengers were heading back to Maui than arriving on Lanai. She started the Jeep and drove uphill past the imposing facade of an upscale resort, the only development in sight. Drumming her fingers on the steering wheel, she followed Ella's directions over paved then increasingly bumpy dirt roads. The Jeep lurched and bounced along, but all the turns were marked, which helped her shed some of that *what am I doing going to the end of the earth* feeling. The sun dipped closer to the horizon, slowly staining the sky with a shade of orange close to the color of the claylike soil. Tessa found herself reaching for the passenger seat as if Kai were there.

He wasn't, of course. There was, however, a Land Rover parked by the picnic area at the end of the road, so she parked beside it and looked around.

"Ella?" she called quietly.

Her heart was pounding, and the emerald under her shirt made her skin itch.

There was no one at the Land Rover, so she adjusted her backpack and walked down a hiking path. And damn, the emerald and pendant must have been sitting the wrong way because the friction increased until she wanted to rip them both off. She was just pulling them out of her shirt when a voice made her whip around.

"So nice to see you again, my dear."

Even before she saw who it was, her blood turned to ice. That wasn't Ella's voice. It was a man's.

Tessa gasped and stepped back, clutching both necklaces.

"Were my instructions easy to follow?" Damien Morgan grinned, showing the points of his teeth. His eyes flared with a feral glow when he focused on the bulge in her hand.

"Where's Ella?" Tessa sputtered, looking around. God, what had he done to Ella?

The dragon shifter purred just as he had right before attacking her in his Phoenix mansion. "Oh, Ella's not here. She never was here. It's just you and me."

Chapter Fifteen

Tessa backed away from Morgan, crouching in self-defense. The emerald burned in her hand, and her mind spun. Was he after the emerald? Could she just give it to him and get away?

It is your job to keep it safe, her grandmother's note had said. *Keep it in the family. If you do so, it, too, will keep you safe.*

Tessa wanted to scream. How was a gem going to help her against a dragon?

Damien Morgan pulled back his lips, showing a row of teeth that grew pointier as she watched. His nose bulged, too, and she stumbled back.

He made a *come-to-me* gesture, flicking fingers with nails that elongated into claws.

"Good girl. You followed my directions perfectly, and you'll continue to do that, won't you?"

She was about to whirl and run for the Jeep when the earth crunched with footsteps. Three men appeared from the boulders behind Morgan, their suits out of place in the rugged terrain. Their eyes glowed red, several shades darker than the sky.

Morgan chuckled. "All right. Maybe not entirely alone. I have brought a few men, as you see. My best men, unlike the incompetents I never should have sent."

Tessa didn't stop to wonder what that meant or what kind of shifters they were. She backed away slowly, calculating the distance to the Jeep. Even if she managed to beat Morgan's men there, they could simply reach into the open vehicle as she drove. God, what was she going to do?

"But I know you'll cooperate. Won't you?" Morgan went on.

Like hell, she'd cooperate.

"As you will when you're my mate."

Her stomach lurched. "I will never be your anything. Get that through your head."

Morgan went on as if she'd never spoken. "You will bear me many heirs..."

She blanched. Had she just been transported to medieval times?

"...and I will reward you," Morgan said, looking terribly pleased with himself.

Tessa didn't want to imagine what his idea of a reward might be.

"Sadly, I might have to share you with that fool, Drax."

Tessa just about choked on her next breath. *Share?*

Morgan's face soured. "The first child will be mine. He can have you for the second."

Her stomach turned. The man was truly sick.

"But compromises are unavoidable as I work my way to the very top of the dragon world. Ultimately, you will be mine, however. And you know why?"

Tessa didn't want to hear another word.

"Because you are special, my dear. One of the very few."

The very few what? Tessa shook her head, trying to block out his words. The man was crazy anyway. She had to run for it. Were the cliffs an option? She was a good swimmer. If she jumped into the sea, would Morgan follow? Did dragons like water?

She edged toward the drop-off for a peek, but even before she saw the full distance to the water, her stomach flipped. No way could she throw herself off *that*.

When she looked back at Morgan, he was frowning. "You're not listening, my dear."

"No, I'm not, you jerk."

Morgan shook his head slowly and clucked. "Now, now. You have a lot to learn about your mate."

"I'm not your mate."

LURE OF THE DRAGON

"Ah, but you will be. Soon. And though I need you alive, I have no qualms about teaching you how to behave. Shall we start with lesson one?"

Tessa clenched her fists, trying not to shake.

Morgan raised his arms in a grand gesture. The fabric of his jacket tore. Tessa gaped as his skin darkened, dried, and stretched into a leathery expanse.

Wings. Holy shit. He had wings. In Phoenix, she'd barely glimpsed them. Having them right in front of her in the broad light of day was entirely different, somehow. She hurried backward, putting as much distance between them as she could.

Morgan was taller than her, but those few inches became a few feet as he lengthened and puffed out a chest armored with scales. His pants ripped, too, and he shook off the scraps of fabric with bent limbs that ended in claws.

"Lesson one," he growled in a deep, resonating voice. "Do not anger your dragon master, or he shall show you fire."

All dragon now, he opened his mouth and let out a plume of red-hot flames. They swirled and stretched, cutting halfway into the ten yards separating Tessa from Morgan.

She jerked backward and fell flat on her rear then scrambled to her feet, moving parallel to the cliff.

The dragon's eyes glowed brighter, and he showed his fangs. Huge, pointy fangs that flashed a brilliant white against the deep copper of his skin.

"But, my dear," he admonished in that strange, choked voice — the last remnant of his human side, forcing its way through his dragon's snout. "That is only a tiny little fire. You'll have to get used to more if you want to live with me."

She didn't want to see more, and she sure as hell didn't want to live with him. She wanted to slip back into her old life and pretend this nightmare wasn't happening. Better yet, she wanted to teleport herself into a fantasy life with a good dragon — Kai.

But, shit. That wasn't Kai before her. It was a very angry dragon, and he was inhaling deeply, ready for another blast.

Morgan shot an even bigger flame, and it left his mouth so fast, shooting right for her, that all Tessa could do was block her face by throwing her hand up — the hand clutching the emerald. It was a flimsy defense, and she winced, preparing for the agony of a searing burn. But all she felt was a hard shove that pushed her three steps back.

She stared at Morgan, but his huge dragon jaw had dropped, too. They both watched the flames bounce away and sear the ground with a hiss.

Tessa blinked at the emerald. Whoa. Had Morgan missed, or had the flames really just bounced back?

Morgan's eyes glittered with fury. He inhaled deeply, preparing for another fire spurt while Tessa backed away. The dragon pulled back his head and thrust forward, casting an even bigger burst of flame that roared through the air, crackling and hissing.

"No!" Tessa screamed, shielding her face.

The air around her grew unbearably hot, but a moment later, the temperature dropped as if she'd stepped away from a roaring fireplace. She peered up. The earth around her was singed, and the emerald glowed in her hand, but she was untouched.

"The Lifestone," Morgan breathed. "The real thing."

"The Lifestone," one of his men echoed.

Tessa stared at the emerald. The whatstone?

Now you are the guardian of this great gift from our ancestors, her grandmother's note had said.

Tessa gulped. She didn't know anything about being a guardian. If anything, the stone had protected her.

Perhaps it will reawaken the way the legends say...

Her hand trembled as she glanced from the gem to the seething dragon just ten yards away.

"One of the five," Morgan whispered to himself. His eyes glassed over with greed.

Wisps of smoke streamed from Morgan's nostrils. The men behind him started to shift, too — two into dragons, and the third into something massive and furry. A wolf? A bear?

Tessa eyed the cliff then the distance to the Jeep. The emerald might allow her to repel fire, but she doubted it could repel five sets of claws if the shifters took her by brute force. How could she possibly get away?

Morgan grinned, dragging his greedy gaze over her body. "Thank you, my dear. Now I profit doubly. I win myself a breeding female as well as a gem. Perhaps you have the other four, as well?

She had no idea what he was talking about. "Other four what?"

"The other four Spirit Stones, my dear. Where have you been keeping them?"

She shook her head. "I don't know what you're talking about."

"No? Truly?" He cocked his head while the other shifters spread out, surrounding her. The dragons moved with skipping little fly-hops along the ground, and the wolf — yes, it was a wolf, and nowhere near as friendly as Boone — kept close to the ground, swishing his tail.

Morgan stretched to his full height and gnashed his teeth, all too much like a fire-breathing Tyrannosaurus Rex. Tessa yanked her necklaces off to be able to wield the emerald more freely. She ducked and held up both stones — the placeholder, as her grandmother had called it, and the real thing — as Morgan blasted her with another plume of fire.

Apparently, he'd been holding back before, hurling little baby spits her way. This was an inferno, and even holding up the emerald as a shield, Tessa was knocked clear off her feet. She lay trapped in a thick veil of flames, gasping for air within the heart of the fire.

"Give it to me," Morgan boomed, cutting off his fire and motioning with six-inch claws.

Tessa rolled to her feet and took a step toward the Jeep. Another dragon hopped into her path, puffing a lick of fire in warning.

She gulped and separated the two pendants, hiding one in each hand.

It is your job to keep it safe. Keep it in the family. If you do so, it, too, will keep you safe.

Tessa took a deep breath. These men — these monsters — had her surrounded. There was no way she could escape. Unless. . .

She brought her right hand to her mouth, kissed the pendant, then clutched it even harder and closed her eyes in a silent prayer.

I'm so sorry, Grandma. I don't want to let go of this, but there's no other way.

"Give it to me," Morgan hissed, taking a step closer.

Tessa summoned all her strength and let herself get angry. Really angry. "You want this stone? You can have it," she yelled, challenging her foe. Then she turned, facing the sea, and brought her arm back to throw.

"No!" Morgan roared.

She arced her arm forward, putting her whole body into the throw. A flash of brilliant green soared through the air.

"You fool!" Morgan screamed, following it with his eyes.

The other dragons and the wolf did the same, while Tessa sprinted for the Jeep.

"You, get her!" Morgan shouted. "You and you, follow me."

Voices grunted. Claws scraped the dry earth. The air pulsed with beating wings. Tessa looked over her shoulder just in time to see Morgan and the other two dragons leap off the edge of the cliff in pursuit of the stone. They folded their wings, ready to dive-bomb into the sea.

The wolf watched them, too, then turned its restless eyes on her.

Tessa's sandals scraped over the soil, and prickly shrubs scratched her legs. Her ears buzzed — an aftereffect of being blasted at from close range by fire, perhaps, but she didn't care. All that mattered was somehow getting away.

She pumped her arms and leaned forward, fighting for every bit of speed. The emerald cut into her palm, and she made a thousand vows to fight to the death over it. It seemed that important, somehow. That critical.

It will keep you safe.

She was still reeling from the way the stone had repelled fire. But something told her it wouldn't do much against the three-inch fangs of that werewolf.

Wolf shifter, Boone's voice echoed in her mind.

In her desperation, she nearly laughed. Funny to think how much of the shifter world she'd internalized in such a short time.

The soft footfalls of the wolf grew louder, but so did the buzzing sound in her ears — and that grew exponentially. Like a huge mosquito, rushing toward her.

The air pressure dropped behind her, and a pair of wolf jaws clacked. She screamed, darting forward as something tugged on her shirt. Make that, something *jerked* on her shirt, tearing at the fabric. The wolf. The wolf was that close. Close, and opening his jaws again, leaping at her.

"No!" she screamed as she tripped.

The wolf came for her, showing off his huge jaws, telling her it was the end. But just as he was about to attack, his head jerked to the right.

Zoom! A huge shape hurtled out of the sky, bowling the wolf over.

The thunderous buzz changed sound as it passed. Tessa pushed her hair out of her eyes and stared.

A helicopter. Holy shit. Did Morgan have helicopters at his disposal, too?

She gasped in realization. "Kai!"

Move to the side! his voice cried in her mind.

She rolled, still clutching the emerald as the sound of the helicopter changed again. It looped around and came back for a second pass just as the wolf leaped for her legs.

Duck! Kai yelled.

She yelped and jumped clear as the rotor whirred over her head. The skids passed just inches behind her body. They clipped the wolf and tumbled him over and over in a blur. Tessa backed away, watching Kai slow the helicopter enough to force the wolf back, step by step, until it turned and ran for its life.

"Get in! Get in!" Kai yelled, motioning toward the helicopter.

Tessa ran and jumped in while he was still hovering an inch over the ground. The second she was in, Kai took off. Tessa pulled herself into the front passenger seat, fumbled the seat belt on, and stared as the ground rushed by.

"Are you okay?" Kai cried, touching her arm.

Okay? She'd nearly been mauled by a werewolf and beheaded by the rotors of his helicopter. No, she wasn't okay. She thumped Kai on the arm. "You could have killed me with this thing."

He laughed. "That's my Tessa. Now, hang on."

That's my Tessa. Her whole body warmed and relaxed — for half a second, at least. Then Kai pushed the joystick forward, making the helicopter rush forward at an angle. For the first stomach-churning minute, the ground blurred past, barely a yard away. Tessa clutched at her seat until the helicopter gained altitude and straightened out, when she finally worked up the courage to reach out and slide the door shut.

She looked back at the cliffs. One dragon dove into the sea while another emerged, shaking water off its wings.

"What are they after?" Kai asked, shouting over the engine.

Tessa gulped and tightened her hand around the emerald. A moment of truth, because Morgan's dragon eyes had glazed over with greed the moment he laid eyes on the gem. Would Kai do the same? Would he care more about the gem than her?

Shiny things, precious things, Boone had said. *No sooner does a dragon have one than he wants another.*

Would Kai lose his interest in her when he saw the gem?

"Tessa, what are they looking for?" Kai asked.

She pulled in a few steadying breaths then held up her hand.

"This," she said, revealing the emerald. "They're looking for this."

Kai stared at the gem, then jerked the helicopter back on course. "Holy shit."

She sat perfectly still, waiting for his eyes to glaze over with greed. But Kai just reached for her hand — her left hand, the one without the emerald — and squeezed it. "Are you okay?"

His eyes stayed trained on her face, and the wobble in his voice told her all she needed to know.

"Kai, look. Do you know what this is?"

He glanced at the gem briefly, then looked back at her, nodding. "The Lifestone. What do I care about it if you're not okay? Did they hurt you?"

Tessa let out a long, slow breath and shook her head. No, Morgan hadn't hurt her. And, yes, Kai really cared. She pulled his hand closer and brushed a kiss over his knuckles — and ended up hanging on a little longer than she'd intended.

Mate, a little voice whispered in the back of her mind. A woman's voice, ancient, feminine, and wise. *This man is your mate.*

The emerald glowed in her hand and warmed her skin.

"I'm okay," she murmured. But her hand was trembling, and cold fear sliced into her belly now that she had time to consider what had just happened. She'd been attacked by a trio of dragons and a werewolf...

She spun around. "God, Kai. There are three of them. Three dragons."

The helicopter was already out over the ocean, heading full tilt back to Maui, but it still wasn't fast enough for her.

"Can you outfly them?" she asked, gripping Kai's arm.

Kai made a face. "As a dragon, yes. But in this thing? No. Not unless we have a big enough lead."

Tessa forced herself to look back. The sun was touching the horizon, casting the sky in ever bloodier tones. For a moment, there was nothing, but then a dragon exploded from the water.

"Um, Kai..." she hedged.

A second dragon emerged, and both circled the Kaunolu cliffs, perhaps deciding whether to follow her or to continue their search for the gem — the false gem she'd cast into the sea as a decoy.

"I see them," he muttered as the rotors thundered overhead.

Tessa grabbed his arm. "Are they the ones who hurt you last night?"

Kai shook his head in a no. "Looks like Morgan brought out the big guns. Hravo and Cyrk."

"You *know* them?"

"I know of them—" he started, then stopped, looking back.

Tessa stared as the water boiled and a third dragon erupted from the depths. It shot straight up like a rocket and made two tight turns, scanning the landscape. The huge beast beat its wings, hovering in position. A green glow flashed — her pendant, catching the sun — then plummeted to the ground.

"Uh-oh," she murmured. Morgan had just figured out her ruse.

The huge dragon lifted its long neck and bellowed in rage. Then it turned in a slow circle, seeking a new target.

"Um, does this go any faster?" Tessa asked.

Kai didn't answer, but the engine screamed at an even higher pitch.

Tessa dug her nails into her seat, looking back. She could identify the very moment that Morgan spotted the chopper because his eyes glowed, and he whipped around to take up the chase. The emerald grew warm in her hand. But this time, she figured, throwing it into the sea wouldn't deter Morgan. The dragon was out for blood. Her blood, and Kai's.

"Kai. . ." she murmured.

Morgan screamed and beat his wings. Tessa was certain he was about to chase the helicopter down, but the dragon hurtled toward the swells at the foot of the cliff one more time.

Tessa held her breath. Surely, he'd break his neck entering the water at that speed and height. Hopefully. . .

The other two dragons circled, and over the next minute, everything was quiet behind the helicopter.

"We're getting away!" she cheered, sure Morgan was gone forever.

Then the sea parted. Water flew upward in two mighty curtains, and the red dragon shot upward again. Closer this time, as if it had swum a distance underwater to gain some ground before appearing again. The dragon arced upward, homing right in on them, and its eyes shone a murderous red.

Mine, it screamed in an ear-splitting roar. *My Lifestone! My mate!*

Chapter Sixteen

"Kai," Tessa murmured, clutching his hand.

Kai gave one curt nod and forced himself to focus ahead, not behind. How the hell was he going to get Tessa out of this?

You should have let me fly here in the first place, his dragon cried.

Yes, he'd been tempted to do that. He'd been frantic, searching for Tessa, but once he'd focused on the inner pull toward his mate, the sensation was strong enough to guide him out to Lanai, right to the rocky point where his heart leaped into his throat at the sight of a werewolf nipping at Tessa's heels. But he had to bring her home, and he figured she might not be ready for a flight on his back — not to mention the risks of flying around in daylight in dragon form. That, and his arm was still sore from the fight. So he'd come with the chopper, just in case.

He considered his options, like ditching the chopper, shifting in midair, and fighting Morgan. God, he was itching to do just that. But even if he could catch Tessa before either of them hit the water, he couldn't fight with Tessa on his back.

He glanced back. No way could he circle around to drop her off on Lanai. Not with a wolf shifter on the prowl. And Maui... Crap. Maui was too far away. Morgan, Hravo, and Cyrk would catch up before that — one ruthless maniac and two seasoned mercenaries. The three scouts he'd faced the previous night were nothing compared to these.

He doused the helicopter's navigation lights and clamped his teeth together. The setting sun shone on a sharp ridgeline ahead. One side was glowing blood red, the other side cast into darkness.

"Molokini," he murmured.

"What?" Tessa cried.

"Molokini. The little island over there. The crescent-shaped one." He pointed. "I think we can make it there."

Tessa, he could tell, was biting back something like, *You think?* She sputtered for a moment and then spoke in an even voice.

"Okay. Molokini. And then what?" she asked.

The woman was amazing.

Make that, my mate is amazing, his dragon said.

He let out a puff of air and stalled before answering. "I'll figure it out on the way."

She sat, stiff and quiet, clutching the sides of her seat. The dark sea rushed beneath them, the wavetops shining in silvery-white flashes. It was the kind of evening he'd love to take Tessa out for a pleasure glide, if only they didn't have three death-dealing dragons in hot pursuit.

Forget about giving her a ride. Someday we'll teach her how to fly, his dragon said.

He wished. God, how he wished that someday, she'd accept him as her mate and allow him to turn her into a dragon shifter, too.

Kai glanced back, calculating how much time he had left. He'd make it to Molokini before the three dragons, but not by much. And then what?

Then we fight for our lives. For our mate's life, his dragon snarled.

"The stone. It made the fire bounce back," Tessa said, holding up the gem in her hand.

He nodded. "The Lifestone."

"What else can it do? It can't help me breathe fire, can it?" She gave him a crooked smile.

Kai bit his tongue. Was she ready for the truth?

You're part dragon, Tessa. Mate with me, and you'll be able to fly and breathe fire, too.

But did she want those things? His mother had never dared.

Tessa sighed, giving up on the idea — unlike him. "Silas isn't around, is he?"

148

Kai shook his head. "He left before I realized you'd gone — catching a flight to Oahu to track down the dragon I fought last night."

Tessa clutched his arm and peered around. "There are more?"

"I killed two and chased the third one off." And somehow, he'd find a way to eliminate these three, too.

Tessa waited for him to say more, but he figured he'd spare her the details.

"God, I've messed everything up," she said, knotting her fingers. "I should never have left Koa Point."

Kai shifted in his seat. "Why did you leave, Tessa? Why? Was it me?"

"No!" she cried immediately. "I got a message from Ella — well, I thought it was Ella — telling me I had to meet her right away. She said there was a traitor among you—"

"A what?"

Tessa hung her head. "A traitor."

"Tessa—"

She shook her head. "I know. I know. I was an idiot."

"No, you weren't. I'm guessing Morgan sent that message, right?"

She nodded quietly.

"Tessa, I understand. But listen. Those guys are like family to me. They're closer than family. Any of them would die for me. In fact, they've come close." He cleared his throat, thinking of the comrades he had lost. The near-brothers he'd shed tears over when fate cut their lives short. "Tessa, they'd die for you — because of what you mean to me."

She turned to him with glistening eyes and whispered, "What do I mean to you?"

He got stuck for a minute, because how the hell did he fit everything he wanted to say into the short time they had?

"Everything, Tessa. You mean everything. You're my mate. Destiny brought us together."

"Destiny..." she whispered.

"Can't you feel it, too?" he asked, suddenly afraid.

149

Her lower lip trembled. "I know I've never felt this way about anyone else. I never felt this way *with* anyone else."

He took her hand so she could sense the conviction, the force that bonded them. "You feel this?"

She squeezed his hand. "I feel it. I felt it the first time I saw you. I felt it when we made love."

He let out a breath of sheer relief. "That's the dragon blood in you."

Her eyes went wide. "The what?"

"The dragon blood. Somewhere in your family, you have dragon blood."

She stared at the gem, shaking her head as if she'd suspected as much but hadn't dared to believe.

"Dragon... Wait. Is that why Morgan wants me?"

Kai nodded.

She stared, suddenly alarmed. "Wait. Is that why you want me?"

"No! No, Tessa! I want you for... well, for you."

She held her breath, so he rushed on.

"Yes, most dragons will be attracted to you, but you only have one true mate. Me. I want you for you. For everything you are." He took her hand.

Her eyes softened and she gulped.

He pulled her hand closer and kissed it. "I swear I'll explain it all to you." *If I survive.*

Tessa glanced back and sucked in a sharp breath. "They're getting closer."

So was Molokini, and damn, the island had never looked smaller or more barren.

"Listen. I'm going to come in low. I need you to ditch."

"Ditch?" She shook her head. "I'm not leaving you."

"And I'm never leaving you, but I need you to do this. I need you to be safe. The Lifestone can only repel so much dragon fire. It won't protect you if they get their claws on you."

Her throat bobbed with a heavy gulp.

"So you need to run and find a place to hide."

Her chin tipped up firmly, but her voice wavered when she spoke. "Are you telling me what to do?"

He managed a weak smile. "Just this once, you have to."

"Who says?"

"Says the man who loves you."

She stared. And man, did he wish he could stare back into those green eyes all night and say those words again and again. But the windshield reflected red as a burst of fire broke out behind them, and they both whirled. Morgan was gaining fast.

"Find a place to hide, Tessa. They'll try to take you alive."

"What about you?"

He pinched his lips together in a thin line. Damien and his henchmen would kill him the second they had the chance, and it was three to one.

"No way," she protested, taking his hand. "You can't—"

He kissed her knuckles once more. "Unbuckle your seat belt. We're getting close."

"Kai. . ."

He shook his head. "Tessa, it's your only chance. Our only chance. You understand? This is the only way."

She held up the Lifestone, making his heart thump faster. It didn't have the effect on him Tessa did, but he could sense its power.

"What else can this do?"

He shook his head. "I'm not sure." The legends were full of stories of what that gem was capable of, but only if wielded by an expert in its use. "You need to hide, Tessa."

The sharp ridgeline of Molokini was directly ahead, outlined by the lights of Maui and the last of the evening glow. As the sun set, the moon rose, bathing the landscape in pale light.

"Ready?" he said.

"No," she said flatly. She did unclip her seat belt, though.

He guided the helicopter in, calculating his next steps. Once Tessa was clear, he'd ditch the helicopter, shift into dragon form, and fight.

Another blast of fire erupted from behind, and he scowled. Fire kindled in his throat, and his mouth tasted of ash. He'd show Morgan how to breathe fire.

Damn right, we will, his dragon murmured inside.

"Keep low, Tessa. Stay off the ridgeline. Run downslope. Okay?"

She didn't answer, but she did slide the door open and stare at the two-hundred-foot drop to the swell crashing into the island's fringing reef.

"You can do this, Tessa. You can do it."

She didn't look so sure, but she nodded in a jerky way.

"On my signal," he said. God, he wished she had the training he did.

If we survive this, we'll give her all the training she needs so she'll always be able to defend herself, his dragon vowed.

"Now! Now!" he shouted as they shot over firm land.

Tessa locked eyes with him. Her face was white as chalk, but her green eyes glowed, and her lips moved. Kai was about to tell her to hurry up when he heard her whisper.

"I love you."

It was just a whisper, but it made his heart leap. That glow in her eyes was a dragon love-glow.

She loves me.

He opened his mouth to answer, but it was too late. Tessa turned and jumped. Kai caught a glimpse of her rolling over the rocky soil, and his dragon screamed inside. A long, mournful cry, a hell of a lot like the one his father had uttered upon his mother's death.

Kai clenched the controls, trying to push emotion aside. But, hell. What if this was the end?

Chapter Seventeen

Tessa hit the ground — hard — and rolled down the steep slope. The helicopter engine roared in her ears as she grasped desperately for some hold to halt herself before she was pitched over the low cliffs and into the sea. The rough ground scraped at every inch of exposed skin.

"No!" she screamed when her feet kicked against thin air instead of the earth. God, she was about to tumble over the edge.

At the last possible second, she caught hold of a rock and jerked to a stop with a grunt. She panted into the damp earth for a moment then lifted her chin just in time to see a long plume of fire flash overhead.

"Kai," she whispered, watching a dragon shoot over the lip of the island.

It was Morgan, hunting down Kai. Setting the helicopter on fire.

Another roar split the night as the second and third dragons streaked into view, each briefly blotting out the moon before shooting after Kai.

"Kai," she cried, though her voice was lost in the din. Dragons screamed overhead, and the swell crashed into the cliff below — the cliff she was about to fall off if she didn't haul herself up soon. Only her belly and hands were still in contact with the ground, and she crawled up the forty-five-degree angle one rough, ragged inch at a time.

The flaming helicopter skimmed the ridgeline then thumped to a stop on a rocky outcrop. It leaned toward the water at a crazy angle, then slowly toppled toward the sea.

Kai jumped from the cockpit. The moonlight silhouetted him as he hit the ground running.

"No! Kai!" she screamed as he leaped over the sheer cliff on the island's windward side, out of sight.

Morgan spat another long line of fire at the helicopter, and a mighty explosion ripped through the night.

Tessa ducked, pressing her face against cool soil. Metal groaned and screeched, and the earth shook as the remainder of the helicopter tumbled down the slope.

She lay still, listening to her heart's heavy thump. Had she lost Kai forever? Did it really end here?

Loneliness greater than anything she'd ever felt over-whelmed her. When Morgan roared in triumph, she pressed her hands over her ears. But then another dragon's roar split the night, and she jerked her head up.

"Kai?"

The roar was a tone lower than the others — and a whole different level of angry.

"Kai," she breathed as a massive dragon swept into sight. Yes, she'd seen him in dragon form before, but never in flight. She lay still, gaping. Was that really the man she loved?

His wings had a coppery tint, and his eyes glowed in the darkness, flickering between the blue she loved so much and the red of anger. His tail flicked, and though the entire apparition ought to have petrified her, all she felt was an inner pull.

Mate, the wind whispered. *That is your mate.*

Her mate was a magnificent dragon, and somehow, she wasn't surprised. But was he a match for three equally big foes?

With a flick of his tail, Kai turned toward the oncoming enemy, spitting a long, crackling flame in their direction. The three immediately split around him then regrouped.

Tessa grasped the soil, panting. She could have watched, spellbound by the incredible sight. But she sure as hell wasn't going to sit back and watch her lover fight for her life. She struggled to her knees and immediately gasped, searching her pockets.

The emerald. Where was it?

Overhead, the dragons wheeled and sped toward each other like knights in an aerial joust. A flaming joust that lit the island's steep slopes in an eerie glow. Something glinted green against the dull soil, and Tessa cried out.

The emerald! It lay thirty yards upslope where she'd lost her grip on it. She started crawling uphill, then flattened herself when the air erupted in flames — so close she could feel the blast of heat.

The air whooshed as the combatants zoomed by, darting and dodging in midair.

Gritting her teeth, she resumed her uphill crawl. The dragons were for Kai to deal with. Her job was to take care of the gem.

A dragon cried in pain, and she looked up to see Morgan and his cronies regroup. Morgan's dark red wings beat angrily at the night as flames emerged from his mouth along with gritty roars.

He was talking. Giving the others orders, she realized.

Tessa. Kai's voice broke into her mind. *Wherever you are, stay out of sight.*

Her back went rigid, one vertebra at a time. Morgan was ordering his henchmen to search for her, wasn't he?

The smallest of the three dragons split away from the others and swooped low over the ground, scanning left and right. The other two barreled at Kai, who flapped his wings and threw himself into another counterattack.

Tessa flattened herself again, putting her cheek to the ground as the smaller dragon zoomed by. She turned her head to watch him continue down the long, thin line of land, and then she scrambled back to her feet, intent on the Lifestone. It glinted, urging her on.

Protect me, and I will protect you, the otherworldly green glow seemed to say.

She half ran, half crawled uphill. From the corner of her eye, she spotted the dragon — Hravo? Cyrk? — circle back for another pass. When she was a yard from the emerald, she dove for it and pressed her entire body into the ground, panting silently. Praying she wouldn't feel the dragon's talons close around her flesh and lift her bodily from the ground. She clutched the gem as the air pressure changed, signaling his approach.

Then, *whoosh!* The dragon swept overhead, making the ground shake. Or was that her, trembling where she lay?

A second later, she jumped to her feet, holding the Lifestone. Wondering what the hell she might do next.

Run! Kai roared into her mind as the dragon hunting her pulled a tight turn and came back for another pass.

The sky flashed with fire as the dragons fought overhead.

"Cyrk! Get her!" Morgan roared. His booming voice was gritty and garbled.

Tessa froze when the smaller dragon spotted her. Then she sprinted for the ridgeline as Cyrk took up the chase. The air pulsed with each beat of his massive wings. When the raspy sound of his breath paused, Tessa cringed. The dragon was inhaling, ready to attack her with flame. She glanced back just in time to see his huge mouth open, and—

The emerald warmed in her hand. She whirled, holding it up as the dragon exhaled. The air crackled around her, and orange flames shot around the sides of her body. But there was no burn, no searing pain. Just a furnace of heat and the scream of a frustrated dragon who shot past her, stymied.

He would come back for another pass in seconds, she knew. And then what? She couldn't play dodge-the-dragon on this tightrope of a ridgeline all night. Sooner or later, she'd slip and fall. That, or Cyrk would find a way to grab her and—

She glanced around. She had to do better than simply avoid Cyrk. She had to kill him. But how?

Hide, Tessa! Kai roared.

She shook her head. No hiding. She had to fight. If not with a powerful dragon body, then at least with her wits — and whatever power the gemstone in her hand possessed.

Molokini was a long, thin, crescent of an island — the remnants of a volcanic crater, long extinct. The ground tilted toward the sea at a forty-five-degree angle to her right, where she'd nearly tumbled into what had once been the caldera side. To her left, the island fell away in a rough, rocky cliff. She peered over the edge, all the way over scooped ripples of rock to the raging swell two hundred feet below.

Come to me. The rocks below, awash in raw ocean, gnashed their teeth.

She whirled, spotting Cyrk return for another pass. Certain death on both sides.

Certain death... The thought stuck in her head.

Her heart thumped as the craziest plan of her life formed in her mind. She lowered herself over the cliff's edge until her feet hit rock. The wind had sculpted just enough of an indent into the cliff for her to stand in a shallow cave. She pressed herself back against the rock just as Cyrk zoomed overhead. A moment later, with one wingtip straight down and the other slicing the sky, he flew along the cliff's face, looking for her — so close to the island that his belly practically scraped it.

Tessa's fingers tightened around an imaginary sword. If only she were like the heroine of one of the books she'd read as a kid. But no sword. No means of self-defense except for the green stone in her fist.

"I want her alive," Morgan screamed in the midst of his fight with Kai.

Cyrk flew at her with eyes that glowed red. Red enough to tell Tessa he might not comply with the *alive* part.

"Why should I spare you, wench?" he spat, releasing another plume of fire.

Tessa held the Lifestone up, cowering against the cliff. She screamed into the roar of the fire as it hit with the force of a battering ram, making her lurch. An inch farther and she'd topple over the cliff.

Cyrk streaked past, breaking off his attack with an angry flick of his tail.

Tessa barely ducked clear of the tail then watched Cyrk bank out over the sea, preparing for his next attack — a frontal attack that would pin her against the rock.

She clutched the emerald, but something told her even that wouldn't save her from the onslaught he was about to unleash.

Kai's dragon voice boomed overhead, and the sky flashed with light that might have passed for fireworks if she hadn't known there were three dragons warring up there.

She bared her teeth and faced Cyrk. Maybe she really did have some dragon blood in her genes. Enough to make her want to spit fire back.

Cyrk opened his huge mouth, taunting her. "Try spitting fire, little human. Try."

Her knees wobbled, and she forced herself to take in a deep breath. She would need it when his fire surrounded her, the way she needed air for a deep dive.

You won't survive the next one, a voice whispered in her mind. *You need to get away.*

Tessa wanted to scream. Get away? She'd love to get away. But she had about eight feet to maneuver on one side and ten on the other. That, and the two-hundred-foot drop to the breakers below.

Think! she screamed at herself. *Think!*

But it was impossible to think with a dragon coming at her head on. All she could do was scuttle sideways like a crab hiding under a ledge — a ledge nowhere near deep enough to shelter her from her foe.

"Die, little human. Die," Cyrk roared.

Boone's words echoed out of the depths of her mind. *Shiny things, precious things...*

Tessa glanced at the emerald. Would it be enough to distract the dragon?

She looked up and found Cyrk closer than ever. Her mind filled with its own roaring sound along with the wave of heat that accompanied a flash of her temper.

"Come and get me!" she screamed, suddenly mad. Frustrated and furious, like she'd never been before. What right did that brute have to come between her and her mate?

The dark sky in front of her blazed into blinding light, but she held her ground.

One second longer, she ordered her wobbly knees.

Another second, and you're toast, another part of her mind cried. The human part, she realized.

Wait, she barked again, sensing dragon blood stir in her veins, giving her strength.

"Come and get me if you dare!" she screamed as Cyrk rushed onward, blasting her with fire.

"Watch me, stupid girl," he boomed back.

"You can't have it!" she goaded, holding out the gem.

"Oh, but I can," Cyrk snickered, his eyes fixed on the emerald. His beating wings were so wide, they blocked the stars from sight, locking her in a bubble of flame. The temperature around her doubled as his flame closed around her, groping at her body.

"Try," she goaded him, squinting against the heat. "Just try."

In two. . . she told herself, steeling every muscle in her body.

"Die, little human," Cyrk cried. "Die."

Tessa's inner countdown hit one, and she darted sideways into the sliver of space along her tiny ledge.

"You d—" Cyrk started.

"You die," she murmured, backing away as he crashed into the cliff. His head hit first, and his neck bent at an unnatural angle a split second before momentum brought his body in from behind with a slam. The flames cut off immediately, just like the red glow of his eyes.

Tessa scrambled backward as the dragon's body fell toward the sea. She nearly cheered — but then her heel slipped on smooth rock, and she pitched forward.

She teetered, flapping wildly at the air with arms that refused to become wings. She kept her right hand closed tight, determined not to lose the Lifestone. Waves spurted upward in a huge splash as Cyrk hit the surface, and she wondered if she would be next.

Tessa! Kai screamed into her mind.

His voice was a lifeline, giving her just enough strength to pull back and crumple into a nook in the rock. She sat there, panting and wide-eyed, not quite able to think.

When more flames erupted around her, she covered her face. Something fluttered past the corner of her eye, and she gaped as a flaming dragon streaked by. Not spitting fire, but on fire.

Bye-bye, Hravo, Kai roared as the body sizzled upon contact with the sea. *Now you, asshole. . .*

"Morgan," Tessa whispered, looking up, hoping to see him ablaze, too.

The dark red dragon shot into view, followed by Kai and a long, seeking flame.

"Kai," she whispered, pressing back into the rock.

The two dragons roared and sped forward until their bodies slammed together with a crash that made Tessa wince. Then they grappled at close quarters, wings beating at the air as they clawed and bit.

It was terrifying yet mesmerizing, and Tessa gaped at the sight. Just when she despaired that Morgan might win the upper hand, Kai would twist out of his grip and counterattack.

Another scream pierced the night, and Tessa whipped around to the right.

"God, no," she murmured, sinking back against the rock.

There was another dragon, soaring over from Maui. One with fresh wings and claws that pinched at the air, itching to join the fight.

Tessa's cry of despair turned to a cheer when Kai's voice boomed into the night.

Silas!

Silas? She sat down, half in shock. Never had she been so glad to see a grouchy dragon in her life.

She sat trembling. A week ago, she didn't even know shifters existed. Now, she was cheering one on.

Morgan broke away from Kai, backpedaling in the air. Then he executed a quick turn and flew desperately for the horizon.

Enjoy the woman while you can, he roared at Kai, making Tessa's blood run cold. *I'll be back. For her — and for the stone.*

She shivered, watching Kai race after Morgan in furious pursuit. A moment later, he was just a sleek form in the night, barely visible but for intermittent blasts of fire.

Silas flew after Kai and Morgan, but he seemed to hold back, and Tessa wanted to scream. Why wasn't he helping Kai hunt Morgan down?

Tears streaked her cheeks, and she rocked, wanting to curse Silas — until it dawned on her. Silas was letting Kai fight his own fight. Letting Kai vanquish the enemy honorably.

She squinted into the night, then gasped when a thick strand of fire broke out. A dark form tumbled toward the sea. Down, down, down...

She cried out when a huge splash erupted on the surface of the sea, then sat back, panting. Was that Kai or Morgan who had just plummeted to his death?

The emerald glowed, warming her hand, and her heart beat faster.

"Kai?" she whispered, staring at the dragon circling toward her.

A pair of blue eyes glowed in the night, making her gasp in relief.

Tessa, Kai called, searching the cliffs.

For a moment, she couldn't move, paralyzed by a thousand emotions. Then she leaped to her feet and waved both hands, grinning like a fool even though that was a dragon racing up to her and not a knight in shining armor. But it wasn't just any dragon. It was her mate.

Tessa, Kai called in exhaustion and relief. His chest puffed out a bit as he came closer, though, and his huge mouth curled in a dragon grin to tell her he was okay.

And just like that, she found the energy to smile, too.

She put a hand on her hip and did her best to play it cool. If she squeaked or trembled now, she'd never live it down. So she went with the brassy approach.

"Well, it's about time, mister."

Is that right? Kai grinned, hovering in front of her.

His wings cast the fresh night air toward her, cooling her skin while his eyes bathed her in warmth and love.

161

"Lifestone. Dragon blood. Mates," she said, ticking the words off like a list. "Boy, do you have a lot of explaining to do."

Kai looked at her, a little chagrined, but a second later she burst out laughing and held her hand out. "Come to me, my mate," she called, loud and clear. "Come to me."

Chapter Eighteen

One day later...

Tessa blinked in the noon light. She stayed very, very still on the soft expanse of Kai's huge bed in case it had all been a dream. But no, the man spooned around her body really was Kai, and the swaying palms outside were the genuine thing. Sunlight glinted off the Pacific, and the silk sheets felt cool on her skin.

Maui. Koa Point Estate. Kai.

His arm was curled around her body, and their fingers intertwined. Slowly, so as not to wake him, Tessa lifted Kai's hand and smoothed the skin. Had her gentle lover really transformed into a ferocious winged beast the previous night? Was Morgan truly dead?

Kai's fingers twitched and stroked hers as he murmured over her shoulder. "Morning."

His voice was so deep, so hushed, she could feel it in her bones.

"Morning," she whispered, turning in his arms to come face-to-face.

It wasn't quite morning, but it sure felt like it. A new day. A new life.

The moment she spotted his glowing blue eyes, her breath caught. Dragon. Lover. Mate.

It really had happened. It really was true.

He tugged her without a word and held her tight, making her soul sing. So much had happened in such a short time, but it felt as though years had gone by. Years to get to know what a good man Kai was. How faithful and utterly devoted to her, his mate.

She sighed and stroked his broad back carefully, mindful of the wounds he'd sustained.

"Told you," he murmured, reading her mind. "Shifters heal fast."

"Tell me you don't at least feel sore," she said, pulling back.

Kai smiled, stretched an arm high, and immediately winced. "Okay, maybe a little sore."

"A little." She snorted.

"I forget about it when I'm with you."

She smiled. Yes, he certainly had pushed the pain aside when they'd finally returned to Koa Point in the wee hours of the night when he'd taken her to bed — but not to sleep. They'd made love for a long, needy hour — partly for human comfort, partly out of sheer animal need, bonding in a way that meant *forever*, even though they hadn't uttered the word at the time.

"So, you call that explaining, huh?" she'd joked afterward as they held each other tight.

"I call that proposing to my mate," he said, gazing deep into her eyes.

"Mate," she whispered as joy pulsed through her veins.

"It's forever, Tessa."

"I want forever."

"With me." He stuck a thumb at his own chest as if he wasn't convinced.

"Forever," she assured him.

"Still so much to explain..."

She'd kissed him, turned in his arms, and settled against his back. "Tomorrow. Right now, we really, really need to sleep."

In spite of everything, she'd slept like a log, and when she woke, her body ached in the most pleasant way possible. Her skin was scraped all over from the rough Molokini soil, but the afterglow of intense sex won out, so the overwhelming sensation was that of warmth and satisfaction. Soul-deep satisfaction.

"Knock, knock," someone called from the veranda doors.

Tessa ducked and buried her face against Kai's chest, and he pulled the sheet over her naked body before growling back.

"Damn it, Boone. . ."

"Hey, don't kill the messenger," the wolf shifter called back. "Silas wants you two down in the next hour."

Boone spoke as if he came to Kai's every day expecting to see Tessa, which made her grin. The men were a tightly knit band of brothers, and yet she felt accepted. Well, at least as far as Boone was concerned. The question was, what would the others think?

She hugged Kai tighter. Whatever her reception was, one thing was nonnegotiable. Kai was hers, and she was his.

Kai sighed. "A whole hour, huh?"

"He's feeling generous," Boone said. "If we were still in Special Forces, it would have been thirty seconds. I think he likes your mate."

Kai growled a warning, and Tessa heard the wolf's light footsteps retreat.

"I get it, I get it," Boone called. "Your mate. Nobody else's. See you in an hour."

Kai flopped on his back, and Tessa rolled to her side, squeezing nice and close.

"So now what?"

Kai ran a hand along her thigh, making her blood heat once again. "Two options. We either tackle the big questions. . ."

He didn't sound too enthusiastic, and frankly, neither was she.

"Or?"

"Or you let me show you how a dragon loves his mate all over again."

"Option two," she whispered, rolling on top of him, "Definitely option two."

He grinned and slid his hands lower, and the fun started all over again. In bed, in the shower, on the floor, making Tessa lose track of time and place until she was right back where she started — namely, deeply satisfied, curled up with her man, and wondering if she'd dreamt the whole thing.

But then Kai checked the clock and groaned. "Time to get moving."

He rose and offered her a hand, pulling her into his arms when she reached her feet.

"Hey," he whispered, smoothing her hair. "What's wrong?"

She kept her chin tucked over his shoulder. "You mean, other than facing a dragon, a wolf, a tiger, and a bear all over again?" She thought back to her very first evening on the estate. "Of course, I have my own dragon on my side this time."

He tipped her chin up to meet his eyes. "You always did, Tessa. From the very first night."

She gulped. What had she done to deserve this man?

Kai nodded firmly. "To the end of my days. I swear I'll always be there for you."

She ran a hand along his cheek, then sighed. "What about the guys? What will they think?"

The corner of Kai's mouth twisted upward. "Don't tell me my tough mate is intimidated by those puppies."

Now it was her turn to groan. "Rottweiler is more like it. Well, Hunter and Boone are fine, but Silas still scares me. And Cruz..."

Kai shook his head. "Cruz is all bark and no bite. Well, maybe not literally..."

She smacked him on the arm. "Thanks. I feel much better now."

She dressed slowly, suddenly aware of all her aches and pains — not to mention a deep reluctance to face the outside world. But their hour was nearly up — and her stomach was grumbling, too. When she followed Kai out of the house, she paused on the huge, open veranda and looked out. So many questions. So many things to work her mind around.

"You ready?" he murmured, clasping her hand in his.

With him close, yes, she was ready. Still, her step grew shaky as Kai led her down the winding flagstone stairs and across the estate to the *akule hale*. It wasn't quite as nerve-racking as her first time meeting the others, but still close. Would they accept her as Kai's mate? She fingered the emerald hanging around her neck as she stepped into the shade of the open-walled space.

"Hey," Boone greeted her as if it was just another day on the beach.

Hunter smiled, too, and Tessa had never been so grateful to see two friendly faces. Because Silas looked grim, and Cruz paced the perimeter of the structure with his face drawn into a scowl.

Kai tightened his fingers around hers as she murmured a shy greeting to the others. "Hi."

Hunter nodded, but no one said anything. Cruz's nostrils flared, and Silas's gaze darted knowingly between Tessa and Kai. Tessa looked at her feet. Yes, she'd spent most of the past hour wildly shagging Kai. She hadn't been able to help herself. It was all instinct, all overwhelming need. It felt damn good, too, and had given her peace. So she wasn't ashamed. But she'd much rather keep private matters — well, private.

"You wanted to see me and my mate?" Kai growled, tilting his head toward Silas.

The two dragon shifters locked eyes, and Tessa sensed the tension in the room jump up a notch. She'd witnessed firsthand just how powerful Kai was, but there was a clear pecking order among the men, and Silas was the head of their tight-lipped gang.

"I did," Silas nodded, taking half a step back.

Tessa exhaled, and Boone gave her an encouraging wink as if to say, *See? All bark and no bite.*

Silas motioned to the chairs, and everyone sat down. Well, Tessa, Kai, Boone, and Silas did. Hunter stood leaning against a nearby pillar as if to hold up the roof — a feat she had no doubt he could pull off — and Cruz continued to pace silently back and forth.

While Silas poured everyone tea in that cultured, old-world way of his, Boone slid a newspaper over to Tessa and Kai.

"You made the news, partner."

Kai scowled and held the paper up so Tessa could see the front-page photo of the charred helicopter and the headline: *Fiery Crash on Molokini.*

167

Tessa skimmed the story. Kai had offered to fly her back to Maui on his back after Morgan was killed, but Silas had come up with a quick cover story and made them both stay on Molokini long enough to meet the emergency responders streaming out from Maui in response to multiple bursts of fire.

" 'Pilot unable to regain control,' my ass," Kai scowled.

"I hope that chopper was insured," Boone said.

Silas sighed. "The explosion was good, in a way. Everyone bought the story that the flames came from the helicopter."

Boone grinned. "Next time, I suggest you dragons duke it out someplace with live volcanoes. That would be an even better cover-up."

"Won't be a next time," Kai snarled. "Morgan is dead."

Tessa squeezed his hand. She'd never wished anyone harm in her life. But Morgan, she wouldn't miss.

"Amen." Boone nodded.

Still, Kai remained stiff as if still on high alert, and Silas stroked his chin. Neither looked all too convinced that the danger was past. Kai had mentioned something about Damien Morgan being involved with an even more sinister enemy the previous night, but he hadn't gotten far before the Coast Guard helicopter arrived on the scene.

Tessa looked at Silas's weary face. All the men looked tired, actually, and she wondered how many hours they'd spent searching for her the previous day or how much of the night they'd spent worrying for her and Kai. Even Cruz looked like he hadn't slept well. She'd been so wrong to believe Morgan's lie about a traitor. From the very start, this band of men had taken her in — her, a perfect stranger — and given her so much. What could she possibly do in return?

Slowly, she took the emerald off and held it out, looking from one face to the next. These men were allies. Friends. She tipped the gem out of her palm and onto the table, then pulled her hand away. It was safe here. She was safe here. And what was hers was theirs.

Everyone leaned in, holding their breath. Even Cruz, who stood as still as a cat seconds away from a deadly pounce. Silas's eyes shone so brightly, Tessa feared he might shift into dragon form and fly away with the precious stone. But a moment later, they dimmed, and he gulped.

"The Lifestone," he murmured, pushing back from the table a tiny bit.

Tessa relaxed a little. Kai hadn't been overcome by the call of the gem, and neither had Silas. There really were good and bad dragons, just as Kai had said.

Boone whistled, breaking the silence. "The Lifestone. So the legends are true," he murmured.

"Tell us who gave it to you. Where. When. How?" Silas demanded.

Tessa explained the little she knew, and Silas sent Hunter to the guesthouse to retrieve the note it had come with, which they inspected closely. Still, that did little to resolve the mystery.

"I still don't get it," Boone said. "How does one of the five Spirit Stones wind up in a human's hands?"

"Not entirely human," Kai murmured, putting his arm around Tessa's shoulders. "Part dragon."

She met his eyes, eager to have another of her countless questions answered at last.

"Silas did a little research and discovered how you're related to the Baird Clan — it's on your grandmother's side."

Baird? Tessa searched her memory. In eighth grade, she'd done a family tree exercise, and she vaguely remembered the name. But what did it have to do with dragons?

Apparently, the name meant something in the dragon world, because Silas and Kai nodded thoughtfully while all of the others looked blank. Just how Tessa felt.

"Baird, as in Aderyn Baird, of the house of Cluew," Silas said as if everyone knew what that meant.

"The last descendants of a mighty dragon clan," Kai explained. "A clan that interbred with humans until the shifter blood was recessive."

"Recessive, but still pulsing in your veins," Silas said, nodding at Tessa.

She concentrated on her teacup, telling herself she would not let her hand shake. Suddenly, it all made sense. How

comfortable she'd felt around Kai from the start. The fact
that she didn't burn. The dreams of flying she'd had as a kid.
Her grandmother said she'd had dreams like that, too. Had
she known all along what their family roots meant?

Tessa sighed and looked toward the ocean. More than ever,
she wished she could call her grandmother for a good, long
chat.

"What do you know about the emerald?" she asked, fin-
gering it.

"It's one of the legendary Spirit Stones," Silas said.

"One?" She set her teacup down with a clatter. Morgan
had said something about that, too.

The others had gone silent, too, and even Hunter, the burly
bear, shifted his weight from one foot to another.

"One of five gemstones with magical powers," Silas said.
"Or so the legends say."

The candle on the table seemed to flare brighter, and a
zephyr of wind whispered through the room.

"What kind of powers?" Boone asked, serious for the first
time.

Silas looked at the emerald. "The Lifestone can multiply
the powers innate in its bearer, I believe."

Tessa rubbed her fingers together, then reached cautiously
toward the candle until her index finger split the flame.

"Whoa," Boone said.

"She doesn't burn." Kai's voice filled with pride.

Tessa nodded slowly. All she felt was a tickle. Her skin
didn't burn, and there was no pain. "I always thought I just
had thick skin."

"Not thick skin. Dragon skin," Kai said, pushing his finger
in beside hers. "In human form, it only protects against tiny
flames, like this. When we're in dragon form, it protects us
against enemy dragon fire."

When we're in dragon form... The words tugged on something deep in her soul. A longing, a yearning she hadn't felt
— or allowed herself to feel — for a long, long time.

"The Lifestone multiplied your ability so that you could
repel dragon fire," Silas said.

Boone nodded. "The Lifestone and a hell of a lot of willpower, I'd say."

Kai grinned from ear to ear. "Another word for stubborn." He was joking, but the love in his eyes filled her with pride.

Silas caught Tessa's gaze and nodded to her. "Courage. Real courage. The Lifestone would not have been sufficient without your inner strength."

Tessa squirmed a little in her chair as the others looked at her with a new measure of respect. She'd never felt so proud — or so self-conscious.

"And the other stones?" she asked, changing the subject.

"There's a Waterstone, too. A Windstone. An Earthstone..." Kai counted them off on his fingers, then trailed off.

"And a Firestone," Silas added. "Precious stones lost in an era long past. So long ago, we only know the faintest legends."

"And Morgan knew about it?" Boone asked.

Tessa pursed her lips. "How could he know?"

Kai looked pensive. "I'm not sure. Was it a coincidence that he hired you? Or had he done his own research and tracked you down somehow?"

Tessa's mind spun. "Ella. Did Ella know?"

Silas shook his head. "I finally made contact with Ella. She had to lie low after helping you escape from Morgan. She works for a powerful wolf pack in Arizona — Twin Moon pack."

Boone grinned and patted himself on the chest. "I got her the job, thank you very much."

Tessa tilted her head at him.

"Twin Moon pack," Boone said, then paused. "You've never heard of Twin Moon pack? Most powerful wolf pack in the Southwest." His voice rose incredulously, but then he flapped his hand. "Oh, right. You're human. You wouldn't know."

Tessa made a face. Someday, she'd get a handle on the secret world of shifters.

"Anyway," Boone continued. "They're cousins of mine. They hired Ella to keep an eye on Morgan because they didn't like the idea of a dragon so close to their home turf."

"So what does Ella know?"

"Nothing. Not about you or the stone, anyway."

"Stones," Kai corrected, frowning.

"Stones scattered over time, long thought lost," Silas said pensively. "The question is, did Morgan know? Was he hunting down the stones as well as a mate?"

Kai growled under his breath and tugged Tessa closer before she could so much as think of how much that possibility disgusted her.

"Well, we have it now," Boone said, leaning back with a grin.

"Tessa has it now," Kai muttered.

She looked around the room. Kai was her mate. She felt it in her heart and deep in her soul. And these men were as close to him as brothers.

"We have it now," she said, making eye contact with each man. Silas first, then Boone, then Hunter, who nodded quietly. She stared at Cruz until his gaze met hers, and his eyes flickered with what she hoped was acceptance. Even grudging acceptance would do. Then she turned to Kai and found his eyes glowing a deep, radiant blue.

She felt the heat of his gaze, but she felt something else, too — the warmth of the others, reaching out for her. Buffering, protecting her. Accepting her as one of their own.

Silas nodded slowly. "We have it now."

"What about the other stones?" Kai murmured. Tessa turned at the hint of worry in his voice.

Boone shrugged. "Who cares about the others?"

Silas caught him with a piercing stare. "When one of the stones wakes, it calls to the rest."

The room went silent. So silent, she could hear the sea whisper over the shore, somewhere out of sight. A soothing sound or a sound of warning?

"Um, is that a good thing?" Tessa ventured, looking from one concerned face to another.

Judging by the way Cruz went back to pacing, she guessed no.

Kai took her hand and squeezed.

Silas frowned. "Frankly, I'm not sure."

Kai's jaw was clenched tight — a bad sign. Silas wasn't much older than the others, but he was the one they all looked up to, and clearly the one most versed in dragon lore. If he didn't know...

Boone clapped his hands, breaking the pensive silence that ensued. "Well, I think that's enough for tonight, don't you?" He stood quickly. "And I'm starving."

"You're always starving," Kai sighed.

"Wolf metabolism. What can I say?" He grinned. "Now, who's cooking?"

Everyone's eyes landed squarely on Tessa, but Kai stood quickly. "No way. Not my mate. She's had a long night."

"Whose fault is that?" Boone winked.

"I don't mind cooking," Tessa said quickly, trying to hide the blush spreading across her face.

"No, you don't." Kai shook his head.

She stuck a hand on her hip. "Are you telling me what to do?"

Kai threw his hands up. "Never. But seriously, do you really want to cook?"

Tessa bit her lip. She loved cooking, but somehow, tonight... "Well, no. Not really. Not right now."

"No problem," Kai said, taking her hand. "Dinner is on Boone."

Boone groaned, but Hunter slapped him on the back, and even Silas smiled. "Takeout menus are on the fridge."

"Order something for us, will you?" Kai said, pulling Tessa to her feet. "We won't be long."

Tessa's heart thumped as he led her to the beach not far from the guesthouse. They stood on the shore, and she took a deep breath. So much had happened in such a short time.

"So now what?" she asked as the big questions pressed down on her once again.

Kai slipped his arm over her shoulder. "What do you mean?"

"I mean..." She gestured vaguely. "I mean with us. The others. Everything."

173

"Easy," he shrugged. "You stay here with me. We live together as mates." He pointed to his house up on the hill.

She looked up. That house was something out of her dreams — a lot like the man.

"I mean, if you're okay with that," he added with a gulp.

She smiled and hugged him fiercely. "I'd love that. Will the others be okay with it?"

Kai nodded. "You're not just welcome here, Tessa. You've earned your place."

She smiled in spite of herself, then thought it over. Was she really up to living among to a group of male shifters? A wolf, a bear, a tiger. . .

She forced herself to slow down. Someday, she'd figure the others out. Starting with Boone — who was so easygoing, she knew he had to be hiding some ugly memories. Like the others, she guessed.

"Well, then, I just need to figure out a job. I guess I could probably build up a new clientele here."

"And go to stranger's houses to cook?" Kai didn't actually say no, but he sure didn't look happy. "I have a better idea."

"Let me guess. Something that involves cooking for five bachelors, maybe?"

"Four bachelors and one happily mated dragon," he corrected. "But seriously — you could try out new recipes on us while you write your book."

She stared. She'd mentioned wanting to write a cookbook the first time they'd talked, before any of the ensuing craziness had occurred. And yet, Kai remembered. He'd been listening that closely?

"That would be. . . nice," she said while her heart pounded and her mind spun. She got to live in Hawaii with the man of her dreams, the job of her dreams, and someday, maybe even have the family of her dreams. A dragon family?

She gulped a little and decided not to think *that* far ahead.

"Just nice?" Kai arched an eyebrow.

"It would be great. A dream come true," she admitted, flinging her arms around him.

Kai laughed. "Just remember me when you're famous."

"What do you mean, remember you?" She smacked his arm lightly. "Mates are forever, right?"

"Just checking," Kai chuckled, then pulled her in for a long, lingering kiss. "Like being married, but better."

"I like the sound of that," she said, snuggling closer. "Not so sure about the mating bite part, though."

"No?" he murmured, kissing his way down her cheek to her neck. "Then we wait. We'll wait until you're ready, no matter how long that takes."

She tilted her head back with a sigh as he kissed the remaining tension out of her and chased it over the horizon.

"So good," she murmured.

"Good?" His next kiss went to the hollow of her neck and ended with a light scrape of teeth that turned every nerve in her body on.

She groaned, it felt that good. So good, the sound of the sea amplified in her ears as she wiggled her body against Kai's.

"Really good. More. Please."

When he nipped her lightly, her blood surged. Dragon blood, maybe, assuring her how good a mating bite would feel. Even giving her ideas about how to plant her own bite on Kai's neck.

"So how exactly does this mating thing go?" she murmured as he kissed her collarbone.

"First, I take you to my lair and show you how a dragon loves his mate."

She giggled. "You already showed me that, I think."

"It gets better."

"Even better?" She snaked a leg up his thigh.

"And just when we think we can't keep it up — that's when I deliver the mating bite."

She arched her shoulders back to give him better access to her neck. Somehow, he made it all sound so good. So good, her body was already begging for it, there and then.

"There's a puff of fire, too," he added quietly. Carefully.

Somehow, that didn't scare her. If anything, it turned her on.

"And then, when you're ready," Kai said, "you do the same."

She ran her hand over his neck, feeling his pulse. Instinctively knowing exactly where she'd plant her bite — right there, where instinct told her she wouldn't do any harm. Her mouth heated up as her dragon side thought about the branding part of the mating ritual, and she had a vision of her big, powerful man coming totally undone.

"I think I like the sound of that," she murmured, already mixing up the present and future. Her body was already on fire, begging to claim and be claimed right there and then.

"You *think* you like the sound of that?" he asked, not quite satisfied.

"I love it. And I love you, Kai."

He pulled her close, sniffing deeply, possessively. "Forever, my mate."

"Forever." She nodded, tickling his ear, then slowly lowered her leg to the ground. "Now take me home and show me your stuff, dragon."

"Are you telling me what to do?"

She laughed. "What if I ask nicely?"

He grinned and kissed her, hard. "I like the sound of that." Then he took her hand and led her uphill.

Sneak Peek: Lure of the Wolf

She can't remember her past. He wishes he could forget his.

Nina only has the vaguest memories of who she is or why two men tried to kill her one terrifying night. All she knows is how quickly she's falling in love with her rescuer — a man with secrets of his own. With her, he's kind, gentle, and fun — but there's a ferocious, animal side to Boone and the group of Special Forces vets he shares an exclusive seaside estate with. Can Boone help her uncover the past before the killers catch up with her? Or will an unexpected twist of fate steal her only chance at true love?

If fate were to come knocking on the door of Boone Hawthorne's beach bungalow, he'd shove it right back into the sea — especially if it started whispering any nonsense about destined mates. But one night, a woman washes up on his private stretch of beach. Before the wolf shifter knows it, he's breaking every personal rule for her and making promises he's not sure he can keep. Investigating Nina's past means crossing paths with a powerful archenemy, cutthroat criminals, and a ruthlessly selfish ex-lover who will stop at nothing to get Boone back in her bed. Can he solve the mystery of Nina's identity while protecting her — without risking his own heart?

The action, suspense, and romance of Aloha Shifters continues in Book 2, LURE OF THE WOLF. Get your copy today!

Lure of the Wolf — Chapter 1

"No!"

Nina screamed, but that didn't stop the thick arms that grappled with her. A second later, she was airborne.

She flailed helplessly before hitting the water, closing her mouth too late. Salt water choked her, and an invisible weight yanked her body into the depths of the Pacific. She kicked toward the moonlight, desperate for air.

When she broke through the surface, gulping desperately, her long brown hair covered her face. She pushed at the tangles and coughed so hard, it hurt.

"Wait! Help!" she managed to scream.

A bad idea — attracting the attention of the men who'd just pushed her off the boat. They wanted her dead, but she couldn't quite process that thought. Why would anyone want to kill her? What had she done?

"Get her," one of the men grunted.

And, *bang!* Something flat and solid smashed the water right beside her head.

Move it, fast! A voice in the back of her mind yelled. Those men were swatting at her with an oar — and aiming for her head. *They want you dead. Get away!*

She paddled frantically. How was she supposed to get away? The lights that dotted Maui's shoreline were faint and distant. The only boat in sight was the sleek white motor yacht she'd just been shoved off. *Angel's* something — she could see the name embossed across the stern in gold.

She kicked backwards as the oar hit the water again and again, thrusting at her like a club. It glanced off her arm, and she choked in pain.

"Get her! Hurry up. Get her!" one man urged the other.

The oar slammed into her shoulder, and she screamed in pain. The flat of it glanced off the side of her head when they pulled it back, and her vision blurred.

"Get her," she heard the man yell again, but his voice was distant and fading away.

If you black out now, you will die, the inner voice screamed. *Dive! Now! Go!*

Nina didn't dive so much as sink. The water muffled all sound, and salt stung in her eyes. Which way was up? Which way was down?

Moonlight filtered through the water, and though instinct told her to kick toward it, she paddled sideways before surfacing again. The breath she inhaled drew in as much water as air, and she sputtered wildly.

"She's over there!" one of the men shouted.

She wanted to scream, to cry. There had to be some mistake. But she could barely breathe, let alone speak, so all she managed was a garbled moan.

"Forget it," the other muttered. "No way will she make it all the way to shore. We're three miles out."

He was right, and she knew it. The ocean was relatively still, but land was miles away. Her clothes were soaked, her limbs stiff. Her head throbbed, and her vision was blurry.

Do something! Now! instinct screamed as the motorboat powered up and sped away.

She yanked one shoe off, then another. Her legs kept tangling in her skirt, so she shed that, too, and let the ocean swallow the fabric up.

The ocean will swallow you too, if you don't get moving. Go!

She turned in a slow circle, wondering which way to go. Wondering why she even bothered. Maybe she should let death take her quickly instead of fighting it.

You're not a quitter. You can't be. Just like Mom. She wasn't a quitter.

Nina sobbed at the thought of her mother. So sick, so frail, yet refusing to give up the fight.

Come on, make her proud.

She slapped the water, as if the ocean was to blame for the cancer that had stolen her mother away. Then the sound of the motorboat's engine changed, and she spun around, seeing it turn back.

"Get her!" the man shouted.

The engine revved to a roar, and the boat accelerated, kicking a plume of spray of water in its wake as it sliced through the water, heading her way.

"No. . . "

She couldn't see into the deckhouse, but she could imagine two men hunched over the controls, grinning madly.

Move! Swim! Now!

Frantically, she paddled right.

The engine throbbed, filling the air and the water with its brute force. The water around her lifted with the bow wave, and she swam for her life, high on a sudden rush of adrenaline.

Faster! Go! Go! Go!

Water frothed all around her, making her tumble and turn as if caught in a breaker off a beach. There was a deafening hiss, a hammering throb. The terrifying sense of a mighty hulk slicing the water behind her.

And, *zoom!* The motor yacht zipped past. Nina bobbed to the surface just in time to see the bow carve through the water an arm's length away. She kicked backward, desperate to clear the propellors, hacking and coughing the whole time.

Alive. She was alive. Her lungs cried, and her body ached, but Jesus, she was alive. She heaved and sputtered, watching the yacht buzz toward the distant shore.

She tread water, trying to catch her breath. Trying to make sense of it all. But her mind was hazy, and her memories were a jumbled mess. Where was she? What happened?

The loose shirt she'd been wearing floated around her, restricting her arms, so she pulled it over her head and cast it aside. Floating was easier without it, but still, it was an awfully long way to land.

So swim. Just swim. One easy stroke after another.

She wanted to protest, but her arms were already obeying the inner command, as if that was her mother begging her.

Don't think, honey. Just swim.

The moon rippled over the water. The hum of the yacht's engine faded away, and an eerie peace settled over the ocean.

Swim, honey. The way you used to go all the way across the lake.

That lake, wherever it was, was little more than a faint memory. And heck, this was no lake.

You can do this. One stroke at a time.

The ocean rose and fell with the long, lazy rhythm of the swell, and she imagined that it was cheering for her, too.

You can do it. One stroke at a time.

∞∞∞∞

Nina had no idea how long she swam, or how far. She simply swam, looking up from time to time. The lights didn't seem to grow any brighter or nearer, but strangely, she didn't despair. Her body was on auto-pilot, swimming weakly along, and she let her mind tune out. Maybe drowning wouldn't be as bad if her mind was as numb as her fingertips.

She switched to her back at some point and looked up at that twinkling stars. Maybe they were rooting for her. Maybe she'd make it after all.

She lost track of everything and faded into a trance that may or may not have been death tugging on her toes. One minute, she was dreaming about dolphins, and the next, her hand closed over coarse, gritty sand. She kicked feebly, wondering why she wasn't moving anymore, then closed her eyes. Let death take her. She didn't care any more.

"Hey!" a deep voice reached her groggy mind.

A wave swished over sand, and she flexed her fingers. Sand? She blinked. It was still night, but darker than before — so late, that the moon had set. Pebbly bits of coral jutted into her belly, and her head ached. Her shoulder, too.

182

"Hey, you can't be here," the voice said again. A deep, resounding voice that stroked her skin and warmed her threadbare nerves.

She lifted her head, blinking, but dropped it back to the sand a second later. Just that small movement made her head swim.

She wanted to say something like, *I'll be out of here as soon as I can lift more than a finger,* but all that came out was a groan.

Two bare feet lined up inches from her face, and the man spoke again, more quietly this time.

"Lady, are you okay?"

She laughed, which came out as a cackling kind of moan. No, she was not okay. Not by a long shot.

"I hate to say it, but this is private property. No trespassing. Which means..."

She let his voice fade away. What did it matter if she trespassed? She was alive.

He touched her shoulder, and she hummed. In light of what had just transpired, she ought to have panicked at being so close to a stranger, but all she felt was warmth and hope. As if her mother were coming to take care of her and everything would be okay.

The man turned her gently, and a warm hand touched her brow.

"Jesus, what happened?"

Funny, she wanted to ask the same thing.

She murmured something incomprehensible and tipped her head back. God, he smelled good. Or did the whole beach smell like sandalwood and Old Spice?

"Can you hear me?" he asked, kneeling over her.

She tried to nod, but couldn't. Her nerve endings were firing blanks, and she was tired. So, so tired.

"Does this hurt?" he asked, touching her arm.

It had until he touched it. Then all she felt was a cozy, enveloping heat. A sense of security.

"Hang on," he whispered, sliding his hands under her body.

183

She held her breath, wondering if her nightmare was about to get worse.

"Don't hurt me," she said, curling up into a ball.

"I won't hurt you," he whispered, and God, it sounded so sincere.

"Promise," she insisted, though her voice was weak. It was childish, really, because he could break his promise. Men did that all the time.

He paused for what seemed like an awfully long time and panic crept in toward her again. Was he going to hurt her? Rape her? Smash her over the head?

"I promise I won't hurt you." His voice was soft. Impossibly soft and kind. "Okay?"

"Okay," she mumbled like a sleepy child — or a woman about to pass out.

Her senses had been drifting in and out, but the second he scooped her effortlessly off the sand and cradled her against his chest, she felt wide awake.

She looked up and blinked into his eyes. Dark, indigo eyes that glowed and flared like hot coals, framed by the rugged features of the world's most handsome man. Which had to mean she was hallucinating — but heck, hallucinating was better than facing the ugly truth. Maybe she'd go with it a little longer. She'd pretend that this was her dream man coming to her rescue and not some hairy old hermit or whoever it really was. Because no real man had ever looked at her with eyes so gentle and so concerned — not one with that much muscle, anyway.

"Hang on. You'll be okay."

Palms whispered overhead as he strode along, and the fragrance of hibiscus mixed with his earthy scent. Crickets sang from the lush foliage, and a bird called. Maybe she'd died and gone to heaven, and this was an angel carrying her toward the pearly gates.

"You'll be okay," he repeated, covering her with something soft and clean. A blanket? No, a beach towel that he'd grabbed off a railing as he walked. She clutched at a corner of the soft fabric. God, she really ought to get herself out of baby-in-the-womb mode, but she just couldn't find the energy.

She stared, focusing on his eyes. Either the indigo had faded to a royal blue or she'd been imagining things. His sandy hair feathered and curled to a point just below the ears. As he walked, he glanced down, checking on her. It should have been awkward, being face to face with a perfect stranger, but it simply felt right. So, so right.

The cadence of his steps changed slightly; he was going up-hill. The rolling sound of breakers faded, replaced by a gurgling stream, and the air was filled with a scent of ginger. Somewhere ahead, a light shone.

"Almost there," he murmured.

Almost where? She tightened her grip on his thick forearm and blinked at a dim point of light.

The hum of voices carried on the wind as he walked on, and the light grew brighter.

She wished her legs would obey her order to stretch and slide to the ground, but they wouldn't. He was carrying her were to a group of people. A group of men, from the sound of it, not far ahead.

"Don't worry." Her knight whispered in her ear.

Which reassured her for exactly one second until he stepped into the circle of light.

"Whoa," another man said, and a chair scraped over a tile floor.

"Holy. . ." another exclaimed.

"What the hell?" a third growled, and Nina immediately tensed. She wasn't welcome here. God, she was at the mercy of these men. They could do anything—

"Shh," her knight reassured her, tilting his arms to let her snuggle closer to his chest. She closed her eyes and breathed him in, because his breezy, salt air scent calmed her.

He leaned down and placed her gently on what felt like the world's softest couch. When he slid his arms out from under her, a wave of sorrow washed over her. She'd never felt more alone or more vulnerable. But then he brushed a hand along her cheek and whispered, and her nerves calmed a little bit.

"Shh. You'll be okay. I promise." His tone practically chiseled the words into stone.

She managed a tiny nod, but her eyes remained sealed tight. She didn't have the energy or the nerve to open them just yet. The voices were frightening enough.

"What happened?" a deep, rumbly voice demanded.

"Get that light out of her eyes," her knight barked, his voice suddenly harsher, harder.

"What the hell are you doing, bringing a human in here like this?" another asked.

Nina shook her head a little. Did someone just say human or was that the water in her ears?

Three men. Nina cringed. She was surrounded by three strangers. Well — two plus the man who'd found her on the beach. The one she already trusted, though she didn't know why.

"Jesus, Boone. What's going on?"

She'd been fading out again, but at the mention of his name, she perked up a little. Boone. Was her rescuer named Boone?

"We need to find Silas," the one with the deep, growly voice said.

"No, don't!" Boone barked.

Nina cringed, almost wishing she'd black out again. Was Silas a bad man? Bad like the men she'd escaped earlier that night?

Wait. What men had she escaped? She shook her head a little, but the memories escaped as quickly as they'd flitted through her mind.

"We don't need Silas," Boone said.

"What happened?" someone asked, leaning in.

Her eyes fluttered open, and she blinked until three men came into focus, all of them looming over her. Big, burly men with inscrutable faces and searching eyes. She shrank back and clutched at the beach towel covering her body. All she had on after shedding her clothing in the water was a string bikini and a skimpy thong. Her skin itched from the crust of dried salt — and from the scrutiny.

They were in an open-sided shelter of some kind — a big, open space set up like a living room. Make that a man-den. A club house, almost, with deep couches and a bar to one side, open to the fresh sea breeze and covered with a thatched palm roof.

"Hey," the nearest man soothed her, and her eyes jumped to him.

Him. Boone. Her rescuer, who wasn't a hairy hermit, after all, nor a mountain god as she'd half-suspected when he'd carried her so effortlessly. He was a sandy-haired, athletic man who took her breath away. His eyebrows curved up when he looked at her, and he nodded as if to agree with everything she had to say. His skin was a toned copper color, and his eyes—

The second his peacock blue eyes met hers, her pulse skipped.

"Hey," he whispered. "It will be all right."

That made her feel better, but then the other two men starting lobbing questions at her, and she wavered again. Everything was a haze.

"What happened?"

Something bad. Something she'd rather not remember.

"What are you doing here?"

God, she wished she knew.

Boone shouldered a tall, golden-haired man aside, sheltering her from the onslaught.

"What's your name?" he asked, so quietly, so gently, she wanted to cry.

Then she really did cry, because she couldn't remember. The *Nina* part came out automatically, but after that, she got stuck. Nina... Nina who? She searched her memories and found them horrifyingly blank, like a photo negative left too long in the sun.

"Where are you staying?"

"Who can we call?"

"How did you get here?"

The questions surrounded her like a swarm of hornets, and no matter how she tried, she couldn't find an answer to any of them. The harder she searched her mind, the more frantic she became. Like a person who'd lost the most precious thing imaginable, she searched the pockets of her mind, one after another and then all over again.

Her mouth opened and closed, but still, no words came. No memories, either.

A boat...two men...shouts...

But she didn't remember stepping foot on a boat. She didn't remember anything up to the moment that she'd been pushed overboard.

"What boat? What men?" someone demanded.

She threw her hands over her face, trying to hide the tears as if she still had a scrap of pride to protect. Apparently, she'd been murmuring in tandem with the disjointed images rushing through her mind. She rolled sideways, wishing she could disappear into the couch.

"Back off," Boone barked, and just like that, the hubbub ceased. His voice was so sharp, so commanding, even she peeked up.

The other men had both taken a step back and looked startled at the command in his voice. They were equals, she sensed, unused to taking orders from each other. Any one of them could have led an elite military platoon, judging by the hard lines of their faces and their wide, no-nonsense stances. But for that moment, at least, Boone outranked them all.

"Back off," he murmured again, and they did.

He readjusted the towel over her body and patted her arm. *It will be okay,* the gesture said. *I swear it will be okay.*

She closed her eyes and focused on his voice, his words, the only thing keeping her from going over the edge there and then.

"Get me that dish towel," he murmured. A moment later, he wiped her face with a moist cloth. Slowly. Carefully. Tenderly, almost.

"She fell off a boat?" one of the men asked in a hushed voice that the others matched.

"Got pushed off, she said," another one corrected.

She wished they would all be quiet and let her pretend Boone was the only one in the room.

"Why would someone push her overboard?"

"Because they want her dead."

"Why? What did she do?"

Nina wasn't looking, but she felt their inquisitive glances bore into her skin.

"Why can't she remember anything?"

She screamed at herself in her mind, wondering the same thing.

"Shock. Fear. Bump on the head?" Someone went through a whole catalog of possibilities. And damn, every one was true.

"So what are you going to do?" one of them asked Boone.

A heavy silence followed, and Nina held her breath. His hand brushed hers uncertainly.

Help me, she wanted to scream. *Please help me.*

"Let her rest," he said at length. "Maybe she'll remember after she gets some rest."

Rest sounded good. Her body begged for it, and her mind latched onto the idea. All she needed was some rest and everything would come back again, right?

"We have to tell Silas," someone said.

Nina went tense all over. Whoever Silas was, she was already terrified of him.

"Later," Boone growled. "I'll tell him soon. First, I have to take care of her."

Taking care of had so many meanings, but she concentrated on the positive ones. Like the image of Boone, tucking her into a bed and promising everything would be okay.

"Hang on," he murmured, picking her up again.

She mumbled a half-hearted protest but immediately melted into place against him. Her chest against his, her arms around his neck. It all came naturally, just the way his arms fitted around her shoulders and knees.

"All you need is some sleep," he assured her as he walked. "Everything will be okay."

He carried her back toward the beach, and before she knew it, he was tucking her into a huge, cozy bed. She slipped in like Goldilocks going right for the biggest bed and hugged a pillow tight, wondering if she could ever get to sleep.

189

A weight settled on the mattress behind her as he sat, stroking her shoulder.

"It will be okay," he whispered again and again.

Her eyelids drooped. Her body practically sighed. She'd gone from lost and terrified to safe and totally secure. A moment later, she dropped off into a blissfully dreamless sleep.

Books by Anna Lowe

Aloha Shifters - Jewels of the Heart

Lure of the Dragon (Book 1)

Lure of the Wolf (Book 2)

Lure of the Bear (Book 3)

Lure of the Tiger (Book 4)

Love of the Dragon (Book 5)

The Wolves of Twin Moon Ranch

Desert Hunt (the Prequel)

Desert Moon (Book 1)

Desert Wolf: Complete Collection (Four short stories)

Desert Blood (Book 2)

Desert Fate (Book 3)

Desert Heart (Book 4)

Desert Yule (a short story)

Desert Rose (Book 5)

Desert Roots (Book 6)

Sasquatch Surprise (a Twin Moon spin-off story)

Blue Moon Saloon

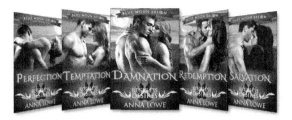

Perfection (a short story prequel)

Damnation (Book 1)

Temptation (Book 2)

Redemption (Book 3)

Salvation (Book 4)

Deception (Book 5)

Celebration (a holiday treat)

Shifters in Vegas

Paranormal romance with a zany twist

Gambling on Trouble

Gambling on Her Dragon

Gambling on Her Bear

Serendipity Adventure Romance

Off the Charts

Uncharted

Entangled

Windswept

Adrift

Travel Romance

Veiled Fantasies

Island Fantasies

visit www.annalowebooks.com

About the Author

USA Today and Amazon bestselling author Anna Lowe loves putting the "hero" back into heroine and letting location ignite a passionate romance. She likes a heroine who is independent, intelligent, and imperfect – a woman who is doing just fine on her own. But give the heroine a good man – not to mention a chance to overcome her own inhibitions – and she'll never turn down the chance for adventure, nor shy away from danger.

Anna loves dogs, sports, and travel – and letting those inspire her fiction. On any given weekend, you might find her hiking in the mountains or hunched over her laptop, working on her latest story. Either way, the day will end with a chunk of dark chocolate and a good read.

Visit AnnaLoweBooks.com

Printed in Great Britain
by Amazon

44202734R00118